CHIFUNGWE

*For Helen Moshak
I hope you enjoy
the adventure
David R Patton*

CHIFUNGWE
An African Adventure

by

David R. Patton

DORRANCE PUBLISHING CO., INC
PITTSBURGH, PENNSYLVANIA 15222

All Rights Reserved
Copyright © 2002 by David R. Patton
No part of this book may be reproduced or transmitted
in any form or by any means, electronic or mechanical,
including photocopying, recording, or by any information
storage and retrieval system without permission in
writing from the publisher.

ISBN # 0-8059-5905-X
Printed in the United States of America

First Printing

For additional information or to order additional books, please write:
Dorrance Publishing Co., Inc.
643 Smithfield Street
Pittsburgh, Pennsylvania 15222
U.S.A.
1-800-788-7654
Or visit our web site and on-line catalog at *www.dorrancepublishing.com*

Thanks Bill, Norman, Johnny, and Les for being my guide and Doris, Paula, Kelli, and Myra for sharing the adventure.

Preface

Africa in the 1960s was a beehive of activity not only politically but also in the area of wildlife conservation and natural resource management. Several countries gained independence from colonialism and others were in the process. The Federation of Rhodesia and Nyasaland was breaking up. Nyasaland became Malawi, Northern Rhodesia became Zambia, and Southern Rhodesia changed its name to Rhodesia.

Independence brought freedom from colonial and white majority rule in Zambia and Malawi, and major changes in social and cultural structure were in progress. A majority of the black administrators lacked the education and training necessary to run the new governments, and as a result many whites were asked to remain in government positions. They came to be known as expatriates doing the same work that they did under colonialism.

With independence also came an increased dependence on foreign aid with all its political ramifications. The cold war between the West and Russia was in full force, but this did not stop these same countries from providing help to what was then being called "developing countries." Canada was sending people to train teachers, Russia was providing fishery experts to do research to increase productivity of lakes, the U.K. was providing VSOs to assist in conservation projects, and the Peace Corps had Americans working in health, agriculture, and conservation areas.

Internationally, the Food and Agriculture Organization (FAO) of the United Nations through its Development Program (UNDP) had been focusing on forestry and wildlife issues in East African countries long before most of them gained independence. Many of the projects were the outcome of several meetings held between the International Union for the Conservation of Nature and Natural Resources and FAO, in particular the 1962 meeting in Warsaw, Poland. As a result of the meeting and after several fact-finding trips to East African countries, Thane Riney, a forestry and wildlife officer with FAO in Rome, made recommendations to the UNDP for several projects including a wildlife and land use survey in the Luangwa Valley, Republic of Zambia. The Game and Fish Department in Zambia supported the recommendation and provided financial, administrative, and technical support to get it established.

The story told here is fiction based on fact. It is about people, places, and events some of which took place while I was a wildlife biologist for UNDP in Zambia. A majority of the information is taken from a field diary that I kept on a daily basis. Imagination and fiction are added to make a complete story. Where I have used fictitious names, events, places, and issues it is purely coincidental that they may have occurred in Zambia or other places in Africa.

Chapter One

The fifties vintage Land Rover was slowly descending the Muchinga escarpment moving over the winding dirt road that leads to the Munyamadzi Corridor. In the dry season the road, although rough and steep in many places, is an entry into the Luangwa South Game Reserve. The local villagers had often seen this old, slightly green vehicle with many dents in its body come through the area to enter the corridor, but it never came back out this way. The same three occupants were always in the vehicle, but no one, except for a few locals, knew the reason for their presence or their destination. Their trip this time was different and was intended to be their last because of the increased personal risk they were undertaking.

Passengers in the vehicle were from three different countries, but they had a major common interest of buying ivory and animal parts from local poachers to take to an illegal market for medicines and aphrodisiacs. The driver was a Tanzanian who was employed to supervise construction workers on the ZamTan railroad project being financed by China to go from Zambia through Tanzania with links to Kenya. He had a slender build because he was also a long distance runner and had competed in several world events. Both Kenya and Tanzania had major shipping ports, and when completed the railroad would give Zambia access to world markets without going through Rhodesia and South Africa.

By agreement the occupants never used their real names and would only talk in terms of partners, friends, or their country. The Zambian was a government employee but was known locally only as a person with connections to the United National Independence Party in Fort Jameson. The Chinaman was an administrator overseeing the financial and accounting sections of ZamTan with offices in Mpika. He spoke English very well and with a somewhat different accent because he had graduated from Penn State University with a master's degree in business.

It was late in the evening when the Land Rover reached the village of Kazembe. The three occupants got out of their vehicle and went to Laston Matshigi's hut. Laston was a local hunter and knew the people and the lay of the land in the Munyamadzi Corridor very well. He was one of the last old-time hunters who had been trained in traditional Bisa methods. His muzzle loader once was carried by Arabs who used the Portuguese trade route east of the Luangwa River. It was now rusty and the barrel had a crack under the hammer that made it dangerous to fire. Laston did not worry about a weapon because his Chinese friend had provided him a usable .375 caliber rifle. This rifle, however, was on loan to him for services. On this trip his friend brought him another supply of cartridges which otherwise would have been difficult for him to buy. Laston often provided local inhabitants with meat that he had poached in the reserves and Munyamadzi Corridor, a controlled hunting area. As a result the villagers never questioned his activities, even when he had outside visitors.

That night the visitors set up a tent next to Laston's hut and they talked late into the evening. They had heard a rumor about an elephant that had a red glow in its left ear. Tales about the elephant having magical properties had reached outside the corridor, and his body parts would bring a high price from well-connected buyers. His Chinese friend was very excited about the possibility of finding this animal and adding its skin, sex organs, ivory, and hair to his next shipment to a buyer in Nairobi. During the evening, Laston and the Chinaman came to an agreement. If he would help them locate the magical elephant and kill him, the rifle would be his to keep. Laston told them that the Game Department now has an anti-poaching unit assigned to the corridor and that he did not know their schedule of movements; information passed on to him took several days to receive because his contacts only had bicycles for transportation. Locating the elephant would be dangerous because the guards in the anti-poaching unit all had weapons and radios and would shoot to kill if they encountered poachers in the act.

"If they find us we will have to do the same," Laston warned. "I can locate the animal for you, but from that point on I do not want to be involved; you or one of your friends must shoot the elephant but not me.

"If I shoot him, I will be cursed by the other animals and I will no longer be able to hunt because I killed the magic one," he said.

Smirking, the Chinese friend said, "We have rifles in the Land Rover so we can use our own."

With a facial expression that Laston clearly understood, the Chinaman stared directly into Laston's eyes and said, "But if you don't guide us we will take back your rifle and use it on you."

"Our Zambian friend knows the Game Guard schedule and they are not in the corridor for the next two days, so we will look for the elephant tomorrow."

Laston had been scouting the north end of the reserve on foot for several days and had seen the magic elephant with the red ear just south of the Chifungwe Plain. This is the area that they would search tomorrow. During the night Laston transferred several small hippo tusks and a rhino horn to a steel lock box in the Land Rover. These items were ones that he had removed from poached animals, and each would bring a good price on the Nairobi market; Laston would get five percent of the sale. When he looked in the back of the Land Rover he saw several canvas bags with radios, two gun cases, and several boxes of ammunition. He knew then that his friends really meant business and that he would have to be careful in making this trip with them.

The next morning Laston and the three friends got up early to start the search for the elephant they wanted. The decision was made primarily by the Chinaman because he was the one who owned the vehicle and was in charge. Laston left his .375 rifle in his hut, but the Zambian and Tanzanian uncased their weapons and loaded the magazines. It was easy driving through the brush, but there were areas they had to avoid because there was a lot of moisture in the soil and they did not want to risk the chance of being stuck in the mud and stranded without transportation on this important day.

Late in the morning they heard an airplane flying north along the escarpment and headed toward the Chifungwe Plain. The Land Rover was easy to spot from the air, and the plane turned in their direction and flew low overhead several times. Laston recognized the plane as one from the Game Department.

"This plane has been here many times this year," Laston said.

Since much of the area was inaccessible by ground during the rains, the Department used aircraft to scout the reserves. The Tanzanian driver changed course and turned east along the main track until the airplane turned south.

"The plane is probably headed for Mfuwe and the pilot will report our location," the Zambian said, but they continued in the easterly direction for a while in case the plane returned.

"Since the plane has been here before, its purpose is probably to check on the location of the elephant, and they may not pay much attention to us since Land Rovers commonly come through this area. If we can find our elephant in the next few hours we still have plenty of time to make a kill and leave," the Zambian said.

With that the driver turned back to the previous road track to resume the search, traveling through the bush to the areas where Laston had previously seen the elephant. Although they had lost a lot of time, Laston had done his scouting well and it did not take long before they saw what they were after. They were driving through fairly dense trees adjacent to an opening and could just make out that indeed the left ear was red in the center. They parked the Land Rover inside a clump of vegetation about one hundred yards away. Two of the friends got out of the vehicle, but the Chinaman and Laston stayed behind. The Tanzanian and Zambian both had rifles, and the Tanzanian carried a radio tuned to low volume. The Chinaman kept the engine running and had the second radio turned on. The two friends got within forty yards of the animal, and the Tanzanian was raising his rifle.

* * *

My heart was pumping adrenalin; my hands were sweaty and not as steady as usual. All I could think of was getting the dart loaded into the capture gun quieter than I had ever done before. I draped a folded towel loosely around the closed bolt and my hand to deaden the sound, opened the chamber, put the dart in place, pushed the bolt into the barrel, locked the safety on, and removed the towel. Sam Mlenga, my Game Guard, was ready with his .375 caliber H & H magnum rifle as a backup if the elephant charged.

He positioned himself about two feet behind and to my right and had his rifle in the across-the-breast ready position. The huge gray rump presented a perfect target. I slowly raised the weapon that was just a remanufactured shotgun powered by carbon dioxide instead of a shell.

The adrenalin was still at work and I could feel the anxiety, but my hands were relaxed and now dry. I aimed a little high at a spot on a muscle, knowing the dart would fall about six to eight inches over those twenty yards. Our target remained calm, unaware that we were nearby; there was no wind and not a cloud in the sky. I slowly eased off the safety, mentally reminding myself that there would not be a kickback, slowly pulled the trigger, and the gun fired with a loud *poof*—the dart found its mark, penetrated the skin into the muscle, and remained fixed. He flinched, hunched forward a few feet, and then turned completely around while extending his trunk upright in the air searching for that smell—and then he charged. My hair stood on end and I froze. Time seemed to pass very slowly as Sam was raising his rifle and took aim. What the elephant did next may have saved our lives.

Chapter Two

I had just returned from church and was changing into my weekend work attire. The doorbell rang, and I opened the front door and saw a blue-and-white postal truck parked along the sidewalk. A postman was standing just to the left of the entrance holding a large fully stuffed envelope.

"Are you David Patton?" he asked.

"Yes," I said.

"I have a special delivery for you," and he handed me a clipboard holding a form.

"Sign in the space indicated." I signed the form and handed him the clipboard.

"Thank you and have a good day," he said as he got into his truck and drove off as though this was just routine to him.

It was not routine for me. This was the first special delivery that I had ever received. The light bulb turned on when I saw the address of the sender as the Food and Agriculture Organization of the United Nations. Six months earlier I had responded to an announcement for a forestry/wildlife biologist position with FAO to work in the Luangwa Valley, Zambia, but it had been such a long time since applying I had given up hope of ever receiving a response. As I learned later at FAO headquarters in Rome, the application and appointment procedure is long and tedious because it has to go through many departments and the selected applicant must be approved by the government of the country where the employee's duty station is located.

I could hardly contain myself. Since I had not received a rejection letter such an envelope could only mean that I was selected for the position. The letter from FAO dated 30 May 1966 informed me that I had been appointed to the post of forestry officer (wildlife biology) funded by UNDP to serve in Zambia and headquartered at Fort Jameson. The envelope contained travel documents, medical forms, an explanation of benefits, a schedule for training that would be provided by FAO in Rome, and a security questionnaire from the United Nations. I had to respond by returning an acceptance letter to the North American Regional Office (NARO) in Washington, D.C. Specific details of the assignment were to come later, but I did know from the vacancy announcement that estimating the populations of elephant, buffalo, and hippo in several game reserves in the Luangwa Valley was one of the objectives of the position and had a high priority. The information would be used to promote tourism in the nation's first development plan and to support a request to UNDP for a long-term project in the Luangwa Game Reserves.

While reflecting on the possibilities this appointment would bring to me, I wondered if it was a coincidence when I remembered an experience in my youth: the first time that I saw a live elephant. When I was about ten years old my parents made a trip to visit relatives in Columbus, Ohio, and my dad took me to the local zoo. We walked around the grounds looking at the usual array of birds, small animals, and reptiles, and then we went into the large animal house. It was near the end of a very warm day and the odor was terrible. The urine and fecal material on the floor from lions, rhinos, giraffes, and one very large elephant had accumulated in the cages to create an odor that almost overwhelmed me.

"Son, we do not have to stay; do you need to go outside?" my dad asked.

Although I was slightly sick, I shook my head sideways to indicate to him that that I would be okay. The desire to see the huge beast and one of the world's largest animals was greater than the desire to leave. How often does a small boy interested in wild things get to stand in front of an animal that weighs several tons and is almost three times his own height and feel safe while doing it?

The cages in the house were small and confining. They were made with thick concrete barriers several feet high on the sides and topped with steel bars that looked to be two to three inches thick and spaced at one-foot intervals. This particular elephant was from Africa and had its tusks sawed off as a safety measure to protect his handlers. On the brass identification plate bolted to the cage there was information about his capture in Kenya when he was young. In addition there was this strange language that gave another name to the caged animal. With only a kid's knowledge of the world at this early age, it appeared Greek to me, as the saying goes, but later I learned that it was Latin for the scientific name of elephants (*Loxodonta africana*). In my wildest dream at the time, I would never have thought that someday I would have direct contact—up close and personal—with distant cousins of this monarch. A thought that surfaced in my mind that day and remained throughout my life was that there had to be a better way to treat animals than keeping them in a cramped viewing cage.

While waiting for the administrative work to be completed for a leave of absence from the Forest Service, I had to get a medical form completed by my doctor and send it back to NARO within ten days. I arrived at my doctor's appointment a few minutes early, and I sat down next to a chair that had several magazines stacked on the seat. The one on top was about health issues, so I set it aside. On the second try I could not believe what I saw: Here was the latest issue of *Holiday* magazine with Zambia written in large copper-colored letters across the cover. Was this another coincidence, or was it a good omen? I finished reading several pages about the history of the country, culture, and natural beauty. The last page contained information about the national parks in Zambia, and I was surprised to find a picture of an elephant in the South Luangwa Reserve taken by a visitor while on a walking safari led by Norman Carr. This elephant sure looked to be in better health than the one I saw in the Columbus Zoo when I was a young boy, and it increased my anticipation about seeing these animals in the wild.

One last item that I had to take care of was to complete the requirements for a private pilot's license. Before I applied for the position at FAO I had started ground school at Arizona State University and was in flight training at Sky Harbor International airport at a Cessna dealership. All I had to do was pass the FAA exam and take my check flight. I wanted to be sure I was capable of flying small aircraft because I had already found information and maps that showed that Zambia had many dirt runways scattered around the country that were constructed during colonial days and several were in the Eastern Province. The Game Department, other government agencies, and private safari companies used the ones in the Luangwa Valley, so I started collecting aeronautical charts for East Africa.

I left Arizona with my wife, Doris, and our three children, Paula, Kelli, and Myra on August 21, 1966, on American Airlines; changed to Alitalia in New York; and arrived in Rome the following day. We cleared immigration quickly because I had a Laissez Passer that the immigration officials were familiar with, and the family had a family Passer Certificate from the United Nations. After getting our luggage we were waived through customs and were now on our own. Although we expected someone to meet us, there was no one at the airport. Reservations had been made at a small hotel near FAO headquarters. It was not hard to get a taxi from the Leonardo da Vinci Airport as the porters there were accustomed to American tourists and were eager to help. The drive from da Vinci to the hotel was about fifteen miles.

The taxi was a small Fiat, and with three adults, three children, and eight suitcases, we were squeezed in like a can of sardines. The lira meter was running from the time the driver started loading the car until he had the last bag off in front of the hotel. Since I did not speak Italian I had to write the address for him, but he got us there without any trouble and I calculated the lira reading on the meter to equal about $5.00. I tried to give the driver this amount but he would not accept it. The manager of the hotel came out to greet us. "The taxi fare is $5.00 each way, and that is what you should give the driver," he said to me. Since he had to go back to the airport I was expected to pay double the meter price. I finally gave him the $10.00 plus a two dollar tip, which he acknowledged with a smile, touched two fingers to his forehead in a half-salute, and said, "*Gratzi*."

The manager of the San Anselmo had two connecting rooms reserved for us; this included two meals a day. When Doris saw the rooms she was just about ready to turn around and go back to New York. Both were small, and the paper was torn from the walls in several places. The beds had mattresses that were curved and very thin. There was no soap or toilet tissue in the bathroom, and all the electric lights combined were equal to about 100 watts. The chairs and dresser resembled furniture that I had seen in my youth in the coal mining towns in Appalachia. This would have been fine except for the fact that it was falling apart. Our bathroom had a tile floor and the overhead shower was between the doorway and commode.

We finally managed to get settled and I left to go to FAO headquarters. The hotel manager gave me directions so I struck out on my own. I had to walk about a mile with some of it through residential sections. The streets were narrow and had so many small cars they almost seemed stacked on top of each other. In many places garbage and wine bottles were on the sidewalks and cats were all over the place. When I came to a main street the cars were going by so fast that I just stood there watching, almost afraid to start across. All those little cars zipping by with their horns constantly hooting gave one an impression of confusion and frustration. I stood in the crosswalk several minutes watching how the Romans got across a street when there was no stoplight. They did it, I thought, by simply being brave. However, once you stepped off the curb and started across the cars either went around you or just stopped. It looked dangerous, but I fixed my eyes straight ahead and met the cars head on. Actually the Italian drivers were cautious of pedestrians and my fears were unfounded.

FAO required a stay at their headquarters to go through a series of seminars on finance, reporting, travel, in-country information, my responsibilities to FAO, and a detailed briefing on my specific assignment. When I got to headquarters I found out that Thane Riney, my project contact officer, had gone on leave. He had left word that I was to contact the chief game officer in Chilanga, Zambia, and he would provide me specific details of my assignment in addition to what had already been sent to me in my employment package.

Because I was going to Africa, FAO required a medical briefing by their doctor who also had the responsibility to give me a year's supply of malaria medication for the family and me. He briefed me on the many diseases that we could come in contact with and discussed procedures if a family member had to be evacuated because of a medical emergency. I was also informed that I would be briefed in Lusaka by the U.N. regional representative on the evacuation procedure if we needed to leave because of political unrest or a natural disaster.

On the third day at the hotel we met the Jacobs family who had just returned from Zambia. They had been assigned to the Kafue Basin Survey and lived in Lusaka. We had several long talks and got a lot of information about living conditions and prices. We heard about the political problems and how many Africans were trying to move into offices occupied by whites and take over their jobs even though they were not qualified or even knew what the job was. All of this type of activity resulted from too great an expectation of what independence was all about. In addition they told us that there were problems along the border with Rhodesia and that guerillas were known to be using the Kafue area as training grounds. The Jacobses had two girls about Paula's age, and their presence helped our children pass the time.

One experience we had at the hotel was when Doris had to wash some socks and underwear for the girls, so she hung them in an open window to dry as she had seen other residents do each day. The windows of our room were on the back side of the building. The wind blew some of the underwear off the line onto a grape arbor below that was in an outside dining area. It was quite comical to see her trying to reach the underwear with a wire made from coat hangers while people were eating just below. She finally was too embarrassed to try to reach the items, so she retrieved them after dark when there was no one in the dining area.

We left Rome on East African Airways and arrived in Nairobi, Kenya, the next morning. Our plane was supposed to be on the ground only a short time, but because of engine trouble we had to stay overnight and the airline put us up in the New Avenue Hotel. Mr. E.A. Quist-Arcton, FAO forestry officer in Kenya, met us at the airport when we arrived, but he did not know that we would be staying in Nairobi for the night.

"Welcome to Africa," he said.

"Our flight has been delayed until tomorrow, so we will have to stay overnight in Nairobi," I told him.

I learned later that Quist-Arcton was originally from Ghana, but like many educated Africans he decided that career choices and salary would be better with an international organization such as FAO than in his own country.

"I do not have a background in wildlife, but in FAO wildlife is under the Forestry Division," he stated. "We have had a number of new projects starting and many in various completion stages in East Africa.

"I just wanted to meet you and your family and let you know that I am here in Kenya if there is ever a need for forestry assistance in your Luangwa project.

"Sometimes it is difficult to keep in touch will all our experts, but I do get to meet a lot of them because they all have to come through Nairobi on their way to and from Rome," he explained.

"If you need help all you have to do is let me know your needs through the Regional Office in Lusaka," he said.

I told Quist-Arcton that several forestry officials had planned a trip to Zambia later in the fall when we had made some progress with our project and that I hoped he could come to the Luangwa Valley with them at that time.

Chapter Three

We arrived in Zambia eight days after leaving Tempe, Arizona. As in Rome, I had expected someone to meet us at the airport, but by now I should have known better. There were no messages at the ticket counter, so we caught a bus to town to check the hotels. I had also assumed that someone would have made reservations for us at a hotel in Lusaka. FAO had sent a telegram to the UNDP Office in Lusaka four days earlier that my family would be arriving on August 28. The bus driver took me to the Ridgeway Hotel, but there were no reservations and the hotel was full. We went to the only other hotel, the Lusaka, that was suitable for foreign visitors according to the driver. Again the hotel was full and we were without accommodations. The receptionist said that we should wait and take our chances that a room would be vacated later.

I decided it was time to start calling someone who worked for the U.N. Being Sunday, I figured that it was going to be hard to find help, but I placed the call anyway. Fortunately the UNDP telephone was connected to a secretary's apartment in the same building as the U.N. Office and she answered, "Susan Smith speaking."

"Susan, this is David Patton. I have just arrived from Rome with my family. Someone from UNDP was supposed to meet me and take us to a hotel," I explained.

"Let me check my incoming travel schedule," she said.

After a few minutes she came back on the line. "You were not expected and our U.N. flat for visitors is full; there will not be any rooms available until tomorrow.

"The only thing I can suggest is to ask the hotel manager if you can at least rest in the reception area until we can straighten this out in the morning. As an alternative, if nothing else is available, you can stay with me for the night, but I do not have beds for five people and the kids will have to sleep on the floor."

"Susan, I appreciate the offer, but this is not your problem," I said. "In the morning you can tell the regional representative, Mr. Gilpin, that I am not too happy about having to wait all night with children in a hotel lobby."

"If I am not picked up the first thing tomorrow, I am catching the 9:00 A.M. plane back to Rome," I said and hung up.

Fortunately the hotel receptionist took a liking to our two-year-old daughter with blond hair and brown eyes, and since she had two children of her own she understood the difficulty of a child not having a place to sleep. She made several telephone calls and checked schedules and was able to determine that the airline crew quarters had some vacant space as one of the crews had just left for a flight. Since no flights were expected until the next day we were allowed to book two rooms for this one night. I thanked the receptionist and asked for her name.

"Pam Stewart," she said.

Monday morning I was met at the front desk by Johnny Kempton, a driver for UNDP. I turned in our hotel key to the day manager and left an envelope for him to give to Pam Stewart. There was some money inside with a note inside saying, *From our children to your children*. Johnny drove us to the office where I immediately asked for a meeting with Mr. Gilpin. The regional representative had left for Rome, but his deputy, Andrew Joseph, was available. Andrew came outside to the reception room. "Good morning and welcome to Zambia," he said.

My anger had somewhat subsided after having a good night's rest in the crew quarters, but I was not going to let the incident pass without registering my complaint.

"After a bad start yesterday it can only get better today, but I think FAO needs to work on improving their communications or they are going to lose prospective employees," I said to Andrew.

"I really understand your frustrations, and believe me it is not what we want to happen. We live in a developing country where time delays in communications are common, not the unusual.

"In any case please accept my apologies, and we will try to do better the next time," Andrew said to me.

He seemed sincere and was not just trying to smooth over the problem. Andrew had worked closely with the Game Department to bring about the project. He provided me general information about how the project developed, but the details were left for a meeting with Owen Rhodes, the Game Department's chief game officer at their headquarters in Chilanga, not far from Lusaka. Andrew called Owen and set up a time for me to meet him on Tuesday morning and told Johnny Kempton to have me at Owen's office at 9:00 A.M. Johnny was also responsible for the flat. "The visitors have left and your wife and children can move in immediately," Johnny said.

"I can cook for you, clean the flat, run errands, and help you get settled."

Of course all this good help would cost me something, as I found out later. Johnny showed up at 8:00 A.M. to take me to Chilanga. We arrived at the office complex about 8:45 A.M. I told Johnny to return to the UNDP but to come and pick me up about 1:00 P.M. Because I was a few minutes early I started looking at African mammal specimens that were mounted on the walls surrounding the administrative complex. Many were animals that I recognized only from photographs and became excited that I would actually get to see them in the wild in their natural habitat. Owen saw me walking around the building and came over to introduce himself.

"You must be David, and it is really good to see that you have arrived in Zambia.

"My name is Owen Rhodes, and I am the chief game officer."

"We have a lot to talk about, so please come inside.

"How was your trip from the U.S.?" he asked.

"It has been a long journey with many logistical problems along the way, but eventually we got most of the issues straightened out in Rome and here in Lusaka," I said. "However, I have come to expect problems, and I do not think this will change when we arrive at our duty station in Fort Jameson. I won't be surprised if there are still some unresolved issues that relate to my assignment that we have not heard about," I said to Owen.

Owen was from South Africa but previously had been with the forestry department in Zambia before he was appointed chief game officer (CGO), and he had a good knowledge of the vegetation and animal problems.

"What were you told in Rome about the FAO project that we wanted to start in Zambia?" Owen said to me.

"I have been provided a general overview, but I was told that you would provide the specific objectives the Game Department actually wants to accomplish. I would appreciate some documentation and details of the issues as you see them," I replied.

"I think the place to start is with some background on the country as a whole to see how we want your work to be part of the government's development plan," Owen explained.

"Our first development plan is now being drafted at various levels of government. This plan considers that the most developed areas are along the best access routes in the country, which are the roads and rails that cover about two-thirds of our total land base.

"The other one-third is totally undeveloped because it is confined to areas where people lack agricultural skills, there is low productivity of the land, and much of the area is tsetse fly infested," Owen said. "Tsetse areas cannot be developed in the same way as fly-free areas since the tsetse fly carries trypanosomiasis, which is lethal to domestic animals."

"How does this relate to wild animals?" I asked.

"Since wildlife is immune to the disease, the tsetse areas have proven to be our most important sanctuaries and they have our highest wildlife populations," Owen continued to explain. "Tsetse eradication is a costly business and is only economical when the cleared area is immediately occupied and intensively developed.

"There is a lack of land pressure at present, which means that very little of the tsetse areas will be cleared for agricultural development."

"Within the tsetse areas, what is the major management problem?" I asked.

"Subsistence agriculture is practiced throughout much of the tsetse-infested areas that do not have endemic sleeping sickness, and this is the primary human land use and wildlife habitat conflict," he said.

"The game reserves that we now have serve as wildlife conservation areas, and they also make an important contribution to the national economy," Owen added. "These contributions consist in the main of foreign exchange brought in by tourists and of more tangible and acceptable benefits to our people in the form of game meat that is coming from our cropping scheme in areas where we have an overpopulation of animals.

"The present Fauna Conservation Ordinance is being revised, and a new ordinance will be placed before Parliament shortly. The most important changes will be a revision of the game estate, and it is the intention of the government to increase the number of national parks by converting some of the present game reserves to national park status. The remaining areas will be known as Game Management Areas."

"Once a game reserve gets national park status, what will be allowed as far as how the park is managed for wildlife?" I asked.

"National parks may be created with several major management goals which might include recreation; the conservation of animals, plants, and vegetation types; or the maintenance of an area in its wilderness state," he said.

"The sanctity of these areas will not depend directly on their economic productive capacity, the most important of which will be tourism. In addition, the material contribution from tourism will be a welcome contribution to the national economy and to the aesthetic value of the parks to the nation."

"So what is your major concern once a game reserve gains national park status?" I asked.

"The quality of the vegetation inside a park ranks in importance with that of the animal populations," he replied. "It is therefore necessary to maintain populations of animals at a level that is within the capacity of the land to support them without major modification of the vegetation from its natural state.

"A high standard of scientific management is essential to our proposed national parks to ensure that an appropriate balance is maintained between animals and vegetation. When this balance is in equilibrium, maximum health of both fauna and flora populations is achieved.

"I think we, therefore, have an acceptable concept, that the sanctuaries not only preserve the animals in perpetuity, but, when the populations are maintained at optimum stocking level, they produce surplus animals which are available either as food for people or for restocking game areas depleted by excessive poaching.

"As you can surmise, the information that you come up with during the Luangwa Survey will be important in preparing a request to UNDP for funds to help meet the goals of Zambia's first development plan. That is why we must get you to Fort Jameson and started on the basic process of collecting information as soon as possible. I have prepared a file with maps, photographs, and some documents that will provide you with background information.

"Also, I think you need to have a good perspective of the topography and vegetation types, so we will plan on an aerial reconnaissance as soon as you get settled in a house and office," he said.

"Earlier you mentioned cropping of elephant, buffalo and hippo. What techniques are being used in the South Reserve to reduce the herd, and how will I be involved?" I asked.

"Basically the culling process at this point is experimental and consists of a crew of two to three employees trained in using a capture gun with a dart. The dart is loaded with an overdose of a tranquilizing drug," Owen explained.

"The drug breaks down quickly, and there is no danger in eating the meat. By using a drug there is little disturbance of the family group that has been selected for culling as opposed to the use of rifles that can create confusion in the group," he said.

"Animals are loaded on a flatbed lorry and taken to the *abattoir* where the meat is processed and kept in cold storage until it can be taken to market. The information you collect on animal populations in the South Reserve will be important in determining the number of animals to crop and whether cropping can be sustained at a rate to keep animal numbers in balance with vegetation production," Owen said.

"What are your thoughts about poaching in the survey area? Is it a problem in the Game Reserves or controlled hunting areas?" I asked Owen.

"The Luangwa Valley is one of the few areas in the territory where poaching has not reduced the animal populations below the carrying capacity," he said. "However, when you are in the field away from Mfuwe, we will provide you with an armed escort just to be safe.

"Johnny Uys, the Luangwa warden, and Stan Stenton, his senior ranger, will brief you on the areas where you might run into local poachers," Owen said. "A significant allocation has been made in the development plan for the establishment of an Anti-Poaching Unit which is now being organized.

"The national loss of animals through poaching in game reserves each year and in parks and reserves outside the Valley is so great that the government is determined that it be stamped out," Owen said. "In Zambia the Game Department and police are both responsible for enforcing game regulations and the police provide us with extra manpower that we cannot afford. However, they are not very effective because they do not take the poaching of animals as serious as we do.

"Poaching activity seems to be increasing in the North and South Reserves mostly by locals for meat to eat and ivory to sell, probably in the Tanzania market that ultimately goes to Kenya," he continued.

"Have there been aerial photography flights made in the Luangwa Valley?" I asked.

"Yes, actually we have some very good photographs. The most recent photographs from 1965 are available, and I will get you a set from the Ministry of Lands," he replied.

"I also believe that there was an earlier flight some time around 1960, and I will find out if those photos are also available. If so I can get the photographs, but the Game Department does not have the equipment for viewing them in stereo," Owen said. "There is also a possibility that photographs of some parts of Rhodesia were made in the 1930s, and I have a contact in the archives in Salisbury that will check on this for me.

"I assume that you would want a set of these older prints, if in fact they are available, and we should know within two weeks or so," he stated.

"Depending on the scale of the photography we can make comparisons between the 1930 and 1965 set, if they have coverage of some common areas," I said. "I would like to take the 1965 photos with me when I go to Fort Jameson and will wait on you to send the others later.

"I want to have a good look at the photos before we make the reconnaissance flight over the Game Reserves," I explained.

Over the next hour's discussion we had agreed to do five things in the Luangwa Survey: build a case for a U.N. Special Fund survey lasting from three to five years, establish a research organization and define its objectives, prepare an overall management plan, establish several new national park boundaries, and assist him with other departmental matters. Our survey team was to consist of two people, but we could request specialized help from FAO when needed. The second person would not arrive for another month or so, and it was up to me to plan the course of action, hire local help, and get started on the survey. The main problem was how to make a case for a UNDP project of longer duration that would benefit the economy of the country.

This would require a detailed report on all aspects of game management not only in the Luangwa Valley but also Zambia as a country. It would have to consider an array of ecological and economic factors from soil to weather to tourism development and all this while trying to understand and get along in a political system that was only two years old.

Once I was established in Fort Jameson I would let Owen know what I needed in the way of equipment, office help, and space. Money had been set up in the Game Department budget to provide just about anything necessary that had not been provided. FAO had already ordered cameras, typewriters, stereoscopes, tape recorders, and two Toyota Land Cruisers.

I asked Owen to give me the names of several people who could serve as tutors for a short field course in plant and animal identification and animal behavior. He had already thought of this and had talked to Norman Carr, the warden of the Luangwa Command before he started his safari business, and Johnny Uys, the current warden. He asked if they would be willing to spend time with me in the bush to get me started, and both were agreeable since they were looking forward to the results of the survey project. The other person was Senior Game Ranger Stan Stenton. Owen could not have picked better mentors. All three would help me adjust to the African bush and delicately guide me through the local political scene because the survey that I was about to start was not wanted by everyone, especially some Europeans who thought the Luangwa Valley was their private hunting reserve.

Johnny Kempton arrived on time to pick me up and take me back to the U.N. office. In the afternoon I spent time with Andrew Joseph learning about all the projects that were in progress in East Africa. In the process he gave me instructions on how my family would be evacuated in case of political unrest. This was a precaution only because the country had been independent for such a short time and there was still opposition that could cause trouble. Andrew also said that Frank Minot, from the African Wildlife Leadership Foundation (AWLF) in Nairobi, was in town and had called and asked to discuss the Luangwa Survey with a UNDP representative.

"Since you are here it would be best if he talked to you, and I will call his hotel and ask him to be here at 9:00 A.M. if that is all right with you," he said.

I met Frank the next morning and gave him a briefing on the main objectives that were the same ones that Owen Rhodes and I had formulated the previous day. The AWLF was an educational institution and provided lots of material for school children in East Africa. Frank said that he would help with contacts or equipment and any supplies that we needed and could not buy in Zambia but would be available in Nairobi, Kenya. I asked if there was a direct mail service for film developing in Nairobi because I had been told that service in Lusaka was poor. He provided me with an address that was a Kodak franchise. They sent developed film back via air mail, and the turnaround time was about three weeks. I thanked Frank for his offer to assist and promised that the next time he came to Zambia we would take him on a game drive in the South Reserve.

Chapter Four

The World War II vintage Dakota left Livingston for its flight to Lusaka and had an on-time arrival of 2:00 P.M. The plane's down time at Lusaka Airport was about thirty minutes. Our family boarded the Dakota and finally we were on our way to Fort Jameson. The flight path took us over the Luangwa River and along the Great East Road, which is a dirt highway that went north to Petauke to Fort Jameson and to the Malawi border. The Luangwa connects to the Zambezi River at Feira where it forms the border with Mozambique. Although the Dakota aircraft that we were on looked old, it was known as a highly reliable plane built by the Douglas Aircraft Company. During World War II General Eisenhower considered it to be one of the most important pieces of military equipment that was vital to the Allied victory in Europe. It played a major role in the Berlin airlift, and many still remain in service, including some in military use.

The flight from Lusaka was controlled from the Salisbury Flight Information Center in Rhodesia since Zambia did not yet have its own facility. However, Canada had furnished consoles and operators for a center to be established in Lusaka, and Zambian operators were now being trained to take over the facility. Once operations were switched from Salisbury, aircraft flying in the Luangwa Valley would have contact with a regional center that could communicate from Johannesburg, South Africa, to Nairobi, Kenya, and this arrangement provided a safety net for non-commercial private pilots.

Our cruising altitude was sufficiently low that I could see the vegetation change as we crossed over rivers and into the adjacent dry areas. It was obvious that development of farmland was not far from water and riverine areas. In seeing this I guessed that crop damage from large mammals would be a major problem, especially in areas surrounding protected refuges and parks. An aerial view of the changing landscape was fabulous, and one could see the topographic features of the extension of the Great Rift Valley into Zambia that created favorable habitat conditions for the North and South Luangwa Game Reserves.

The Dakota made its turn into the downwind leg of the runway, and no other planes were currently parked at the terminal. On the final approach, the town and surrounding rural villages were clearly visible. The flight from Lusaka had been a smooth and enjoyable ride. The nine passengers deplaned quickly, and I began to look for my Game Department contact who was to meet us. The thatched roof terminal had a small waiting area for passengers, a ticket counter, and a radio tower that was staffed by one government employee. A refueling truck and fire engine were off to the left of the entrance gate. The fire engine looked new and had a crew of three.

There was a bulletin board inside the terminal with messages left by various people. One message indicated that a Cessna 170 was for rent by a fellow named Robert Lawson. I took this note and put it inside my coat pocket for future reference. After about a half hour wait, Senior Game Ranger Stan Stenton picked us up in a Game Department Land Rover and took our family to the Crystal Springs Hotel near the airport. He explained that no accommodations were available in Fort Jameson at the government hostel, but rooms would be available the next day. He also said that he was on the shortwave radio to Chilanga talking to the CGO and was informed that we were arriving today.

"I will not be available tomorrow, but my secretary, Yvonne Ryle, will come to get you at about 9:00 A.M. and take you to the government hostel," he said. "There are no places to stay in Fort Jameson other than the Government Hostel and Crystal Springs Hotel. The Game Department has a house on a farm near Fort Jameson, but it is too crude for a family," Stan said.

The Crystal Springs Hotel was a relic of the past, but by now anything with a bed was welcome. One unusual item in our bathroom was a huge bright yellow bathtub. The kids got quite a charge out of bathing in this tub and trying to figure out where it had come from and how old it was. We never did get answers to the two questions.

That night we ate in the small dining room of the hotel and talked a long time with the two South African pilots who worked for Central African Airways. They said that the military types on their flight from Livingston to Lusaka were guerrillas who had recently been involved in raiding white-owned farms in Southern Rhodesia, and they claimed to have killed several farmers. The pilots also indicated that it was generally known that guerrillas were using the areas around Kafue National Park south of Lusaka for training, and the two men on the Livingston flight were headed back to their base. The pilots also told us that the two soldiers were flying on tickets purchased by the Government of Zambia. This type of information started me wondering whether Zambia was safe for international workers and if I had made the right decision. But since my duty station was 375 miles north of Lusaka and not close to the Rhodesian border, I assumed that it would be a much safer area, and later this was confirmed in several ways.

We continued to be engaged in conversation with the pilots for several hours, and during this time one asked why I was in Zambia with a wife and three children. It was hard to answer this question and tell them why someone who had a perfectly good job would leave and come to a developing country in Africa. I explained that to a wildlife biologist Africa was a place to learn and experience firsthand how many species could occupy the same general piece of land and still maintain their populations over time. It was the dream of most wildlife biologists to do what I was going to do, but making the decision was influenced by a supportive family even though it did involve some risk, especially at this time in Africa.

My two-year-old blond daughter had captured the attention of James Hill, one of the pilots. He was also intrigued with the maturity of our oldest daughter who was twelve. I was taken aback when he offered to take our three children to Salisbury to live with him and his wife to attend school. The pilot was about forty years old and said that he did not have children. He was quite sincere that our girls should not go to school in Zambia because of the low quality of education that they would receive. I told him that we had already made the decision that they would attend a local school in Fort Jameson. Even if the education was not of the quality that they could receive in other countries, the experience of living and going to school in Zambia would provide them a greater understanding of the problems, life, and customs of a different culture.

Our discussions turned to politics and I became more aware of the conflicts that existed between Zambia and Southern Rhodesia. As a result I decided that I would try hard to refrain from any political discussions, but as time would tell this was difficult to do. On one occasion while I was receiving an orientation at the UNDP office in Lusaka, I was confronted by a U.N. employee and asked why the U.S. was bombing cities in Viet Nam. As I found out later, this individual hated all whites and Americans in particular. I was told by his fellow African employees just to discount anything that this person might say. He was all talk with no action. Later I found out that he finally got so antagonistic that the regional representative terminated his employment.

The next day Yvonne, the Game Department secretary, came to pick us up and take us to the government hostel. I soon learned that not only was housing not available, but an application had not even been submitted on my behalf. This was after assurance by FAO that family housing was awaiting us in Fort

Jameson. In Fort Jameson, as in other towns in Zambia, each government agency is allocated houses depending on the number of employees. The Game Department had two houses, both of which were occupied. This meant that we had to move into the government hostel, but I was glad that we did not have to stay at Crystal Springs more than one night.

The hostel had at one time been called Codrington House, but in keeping with the policy of eliminating all remnants of colonialism, the government renamed it to Luangwa House. It was situated on a lot about five acres in size with a courtyard surrounded by a beautiful garden and flowering trees, including poinsettias. Our room had an enclosed veranda where we could put two beds so all five of us were able to stay together. All beds in Zambia, as far as I know, were single as in Rome. My English friends thought that it was quite odd for me to want a double bed; on the other hand, I thought they were a little odd to want to sleep in separate beds.

The dinner hour is a time that we have always enjoyed as a family, and I was quite shocked the first night at the hostel to learn that our children could not eat with us. Instead they ate a half hour early, which was 6:30 P.M., and had a completely different menu. All three of the girls had been used to a hearty evening meal, but this was not served to children in the hostel. For dinner they had a delightful choice of either an egg or cold cereal. This was the same choice each day for breakfast and dinner every evening. I did visit with the hostel manager and arranged for our children to eat with us after the first evening—the diet of eggs or cereal twice a day was not adequate for growing kids of their ages.

The first few days at the hostel were enjoyable. Doris needed a rest as she had been suffering from an iron deficiency. This kept her feeling weak, and she welcomed a chance to let someone else do the work. One custom that we all liked was morning tea, which was a leftover tradition of British rule. At 6:00 A.M. every morning except Sunday hot tea was served to each resident. I think the hot tea helped us recover from the many effects of traveling. Although I had never made it a habit to drink anything but iced tea in the daytime, hot tea soon became a necessity for breakfast because I could not drink the coffee.

By the end of ten days living at the hostel I decided that it was time to be more aggressive about obtaining a house. Until now I could not get an answer from government officials as to when one would become available. At this point there was only one thing to do and that was to put my cards on the table, so I made an appointment with the district secretary, Angus McDonald, to discuss the problem. The meeting was short but I had enough time to explain that I was in Zambia for the United Nations at the request of the government. I had been informed before leaving Arizona that a house suitable for the family was available and reserved for us. If I did not receive a house within three days I was returning to Rome. Then the government would have to explain to FAO why housing was not available when they had listed it in the terms of reference. Within two days I was offered a house that had been vacant since the previous police commissioner had changed jobs. It was adjacent to the house occupied by Angus MacDonald on a hill about a mile from town.

It was a relief to get out of the hostel, and the house afforded us some much-needed privacy. It was large, with three bedrooms, a dining room, a kitchen, living room, bathroom, and storage space. The main problem was that the house did not have furniture and was heavily infested with roaches. Hard furniture was later provided by the Public Works Department, and I had to go there and sign for each piece. The roach problem lasted for several weeks, but after using fifteen spray cans of DDT, we eliminated the infestation problem in the house and hoped we had significantly reduced the population. As a result of so much spraying of insecticide I think all five of us had a mild case of DDT poisoning.

We had a variety of flowering plants around the yard that included bamboo, papaya, bananas, and mangos. However we never got to taste many of the fruits because as soon as they got ripe they seemed to disappear from the trees. The view from the front veranda was simply beautiful. We could see the mountains in Malawi in the distance, and I spent some of my most enjoyable moments watching the day fade behind these hills. I often got the feeling that life began in Africa and had not advanced much since then. Living conditions in Fort Jameson varied from time to time. When we first arrived there was a water shortage and it was rationed to two hours a day. Our house, being near the reservoir, was never completely out of water, but many houses did without for as much as two weeks at a time. Several boreholes had been drilled, but it was a matter of distribution and a lack of spare parts for pumps, not a lack of water that caused the problem.

My troubles in getting established and everything ready to actually start the Luangwa project did not end with getting a house. Although I had a valid drivers license from the U.S., this was not acceptable at the Public Works Department where licenses were issued. I was told that I needed an international license before I could be given a Zambian license to drive a private or government vehicle. Not having one, I told the clerk that I was working for the United Nations and I was supposed to be issued a license without a test. He said that only diplomats and holders of an international license were the ones who could be given a Zambian license without a test. I showed him my Laissez Passer, and he accepted the fact that I was some sort of diplomat and then referred me to the town council. When I went to the town council I had the same problem. The clerk there wanted to see my international license. Again I brought out my Laissez Passer and told him that it was my verification of diplomatic status issued by the U.N. He looked at it very carefully with its four different foreign languages and asked where it showed what I could drive. I told him that, because I had to travel in so many countries, out of necessity my authority to drive was written in several foreign languages and I pointed out various paragraphs and told him that was my authority to drive. The clerk finally agreed that I had an international license and could have a Zambian license—but only after I paid him twenty shillings.

Food supplies came mostly from Lusaka by lorry on a dirt road of approximately 375 miles. When Ian Smith made a unilateral declaration of independence in Southern Rhodesia the supply problems became acute. Petrol was rationed throughout the country, but since Fort Jameson was near the Malawi border, where lorries brought the petrol through from Salima, we could get it without ration cards. It was a different problem in Lusaka where rationing was strictly enforced. I often went to Lusaka on business and had to depend on the Game Department to furnish a vehicle and petrol, and at times it was just as easy to squeeze blood out of a turnip.

One of the first things that I learned about living in Zambia was that we would need a houseboy to help with the cleaning and wood cutting. Most expatriates had a houseboy, cook, and garden boy. Doris decided for the time being that only a houseboy would be needed. We had become friendly with an African waiter at the hostel by the name of Maxwell. He had worked there for five years and said he had a brother who needed a job and would make a good houseboy. Most Africans have small reference books where previous employers have written something to the effect that the bearer is an honest person and that his salary was four or five shillings per day. However it was common knowledge that books were loaned and one could not always be sure that the person presenting the book was in fact was the one spoken about in the reference. Maxwell had given me his brother's two books to read and, according to his references, he had worked last for a school teacher in Fort Jameson.

The day Tembo came to the hostel to meet me he was neatly dressed and wore a tie. He was a good looking young man of twenty-four years and had impressive white teeth. His English was good, but he had difficulty understanding me because I certainly did not sound like anyone he had ever heard before. I was impressed by his appearance and figured that if he took the time to dress himself to get a job then he deserved one. I had already been approached by several men wanting jobs whose appearance was quite the opposite. Tembo's reaction to me was, I am sure, equal to mine toward him; I had never had an African houseboy, and he had never had an American employer. I could tell right off that he knew I was different from other whites he had met, and I wondered how he would react to Doris and the children. Over time he came to enjoy our family, became very protective of them, and we certainly learned a lot from him about African culture.

When I took Tembo to see our house he was quite thrilled at his own place. It was a three-room palace as far as he was concerned. Servants' quarters were usually located behind the regular house but within shouting distance of the "Madam." They have no electricity or hot water, and some did not have water at all. Tembo's toilet was the same as those furnished servants during colonial days. It was the type where you have to squat instead of sitting on a commode, but it had a flush system from an overhead water tank. He also had a shower stall, but there was no way to heat water. However, for people who have all their lives been in a village and without any type of comfort, these houses were castles to them.

As I began to get everything together that was needed for a family of five to survive, my attention turned more to the job that I was assigned by FAO. For the first couple of weeks I worked out of the hostel and then my house. Then the Game Department found space in an old warehouse next to their main office, and this is where I would work until the FAO office was constructed. Ultimately the FAO office would become the headquarters for the Game Department when the Luangwa Survey was completed.

The warehouse was loaded with ivory, leopard, lion, zebra, and cheetah skins. There were also confiscated weapons and skulls of many animals. All of these items had been taken from poachers or turned in as part of an amnesty declared by President Kaunda. The market value of the ivory alone would have been more than several million dollars. The roof of the warehouse was thatch and leaked when it rained. As a result there was an odor from heavy mold caused by dampness. Many of the skins were decaying and insect-infested, but no one would make the decision to burn the animal products.

Many of the old files from the Game Department dating back thirty to forty years were in boxes that also were deteriorating. For the next few days I spent time rearranging all the items, opening space to let air circulate, and stacking boxes and paper according to a crude subject index. To provide more reflected light inside, I whitewashed the walls and installed several overhead lights. Although the roof still leaked, the storehouse was now beginning to take on the appearance of a crude but workable office space.

Chapter Five

My first major job was to go through old Department records trying to piece together past events, especially as they related to animal populations. After several weeks of being in the warehouse I was given a room in the main office building, and I began to bring boxes into my new space so that I could work without the smell of mold permeating my clothing. As I went through the cartons of files I became acquainted with the various personalities when I read their tour reports and diaries, some going back to the 1930s and '40s. That was a period when wildlife was a major attraction to hunters all over the world but primarily Europe and the United States. The major goal of hunters then was trying to bag the biggest and most dangerous animals that could be found. This often led to conflicts between game rangers and safari operators who pushed the limits of those charged with protection of wildlife.

One thing that came to light early was that many of the people who worked for the Department in the early days were highly opinionated. A ranger would write a letter to his supervisor in which he would make a statement about vegetation or animals. He would receive a letter back saying that he could not be right because it was not that way at all. In turn the ranger would write another letter criticizing the criticisms of his supervisor. Some of the arguments carried on for months and even years. In later times as the Department began to get a few college-trained personnel to fill vacant positions, conflicts also developed between the biologists and rangers. Most of the rangers had come up through the ranks and were the center of attention, but the biologists were a threat to their status.

In addition to having personnel problems within their own organization, the Game Department had trouble with the other departments in the government, and much of it was still evident even after independence. The district secretary said that the Department had always tried to maintain an air of authority and had never wanted to promote cooperation with other government units. Regardless of the conflicts that existed in the early years and, even those that occurred later, the Game Department of Northern Rhodesia and now Zambia had done a good job in protecting wildlife with the budget and personnel they had at the time.

After being in Fort Jameson for several weeks, I had not had the opportunity to meet Norman Carr, and this was a high priority for me before I actually started fieldwork. Norman was a very busy person and had been out on a walking safari in the Luangwa Valley when I first arrived in Fort Jameson. CGO had already provided me a background of Norman's career, which in turn made me anxious to meet him to learn more about his conservation philosophy, bush experience, and the man himself.

Norman was born in East Africa but educated in England. He served in World War II and was a company commander. After the war he worked as an elephant control officer, but he had a strong desire to be more involved in conservation and preservation. Later he became chief ranger in the Northern Rhodesian Game Department where he helped create reserves and parks and for his work was recognized by being awarded Member of the British Empire. As a result of a back injury suffered from an encounter with a buffalo, Norman had to leave his position, but after surgery he was able to return to Northern Rhodesia to be warden for the Kafue National Park, the largest national park in Africa.

When I walked into the Luangwa Safari Office I recognized Norman right away. His secretary, Mrs. Leach-Lewis, asked, "May I help you?"

"I am here to see the gentleman right there," I replied, while pointing to Norman standing in the doorway to an office.

"My name is David Patton, and Owen Rhodes has told you about me and the Luangwa Valley Survey. If you have time I would like to get your opinion on several issues that will affect my work."

"Actually, I do have some time, and yes I did talk to Owen about the survey. Have a seat and tell me about yourself and what brings you to Africa," he said.

His demeanor and tone of voice was not of the "English" attitude that I had run into in the past few weeks. *This is a person that I can trust and do business with*, I said to myself.

This English attitude, as I learned over time, was normal and not intended for me personally but was just a human characteristic that I was not familiar with. Having accepted this fact I was able to work with expatriates without problems and became close friends with many. One of the most frequent statements made when meeting non-Americans in Africa was that I spoke a different English than they had heard before. Of course this invoked a long discussion of the Revolutionary War with England and who won.

"Actually, my reasons for coming to Africa are many and varied. The opportunity was available, and at this particular time in my life I wanted to have an adventure and do something different that included my family. It was also a desire to see how rural people lived in Africa and how much difference there was in our basic desires for life," I said to Norman. "Also I have wanted to see elephants in the wild since my first visit to a zoo when I was a young boy.

"If I had to identify one reason, it probably would be to see for myself the variety of species that could share the same space for food and cover and to try to understand the plant and animal relationships that take place on a day-to-day basis.

"In many of my ecology courses I took in college, this was always used as an example of niche theory and coexistence of a large number of species. Before coming to Zambia I saw your picture in a tourist magazine guiding people on a walking safari. There you were standing with tourists watching elephants going to water. When I saw the picture I made a mental note to myself that you were a person that I had to meet, and here I am.

"In many of my visits to the San Diego Wildlife Park, I was able to observe elephants in open space, and I was always fascinated by the slow but deliberate movements and the ability of a five-ton animal to pick up tiny objects with the finger-like lips on the tip of their trunks," I said to Norman.

"Johnny Uys has already agreed to be my tutor on elephant behavior, and we plan on being in the South Reserve in a couple of weeks. Before seeing the reserves on the ground, Owen, Johnny and I will also see them from the air so the major rivers and landmarks will be familiar to me.

"Norman, you were warden before you retired and have spent many hours in the Luangwa Reserves, so your opinion on the conditions or management issues will mean a lot in terms of where I direct my efforts for the FAO sponsored survey. From what I have learned so far it seems to me that elephant, buffalo, and hippo are the main issues that face the Department for the foreseeable future. Is this a fair assumption?" I asked.

"Elephant populations have been increasing since the 1940s," he said. "We did not start noticing changes in vegetation until about the mid 1950s when baobab trees were starting to show damage from elephants. By 1960 there was large-scale destruction of baobabs, and browse lines were starting to appear in some areas on mopane and acacia, and this to me is an indicator that there are too many elephants.

"Buffalo and hippo populations also have been increasing, and between the three species there is habitat destruction, and I support the cropping scheme that has been undertaken by the Game Department," he explained.

"But what about poaching? Is it having an effect on populations?" I asked.

"The current level of poaching is not significant in reducing animal numbers because it is mainly by local people who want the meat and ivory," he said. "Most of the poaching now is done with antique muzzle loaders with the locals making their own gunpowder. This type of poaching, however, is still illegal and has to stop. There does appear to be an increase in poaching for ivory in surrounding countries, and I expect that we will face the same situation here in Zambia before too long.

"In the future if the Game Department and safari hunters can hire local people and let them have some of the game meat, then poaching may decline," Norman explained. "My greatest concern with local poaching is that modern weapons will find their way into the bush, and to some extent this is already happening.

"Also we have to be fully aware that poaching will increase as the price of ivory increases, and there is the possibility that outsiders will make their way to the Luangwa Valley because it's a difficult area to patrol with the current level of staffing by Game Guards," Norman said.

"There was also considerable poaching before independence as a way to harass the white colonials in power, and I suspect this has become a way of life in some areas.

"What the Game Department needs is better population estimates so poaching, safari kills, and damage control kills can be factored into the annual increase to determine how many elephants need to be culled each year to maintain a balance between animals and vegetation, and this is where the Luangwa Survey will really be beneficial," he said.

"I have another question. Where are the areas that the Game Department lacks adequate information about elephant populations and movements in and out of the Luangwa Reserves?" I asked.

"The Department has a marking crew operating in the South Reserve around the Mfuwe area where animals move outside the reserve to raid local gardens in Nsefu, Luambe, and Lukusuzi," he said. "Elephant numbers are high in the Munyamadzi Corridor, which is a controlled hunting area.

"These elephants seem to move around the base of the Muchinga escarpment, north to Pande Plains and south through the Chifungwe Plain to Lundu Plain, but we really don't have good information about this area because it has been isolated for a long time," he continued.

"I would think that the general area around Chifungwe Plain would be a good place for a marking crew because movement information is going to be extremely important there when determining the boundaries of national parks and wildlife management areas.

"This area probably has some of the highest elephant populations in East Africa," he said. "How long this condition will remain is of great concern because there is a road from Mpika over the escarpment that crosses the Mupamadzi River into the corridor. It is a route that could be used for transporting ivory through Tanzania to Kenya where there is a growing market," he concluded.

"Norman, I have already taken up a lot of your time but I hope that I can visit you often to discuss problems when we run across them as the field work progresses. You have given me a lot of good information, and there is a high probability that I will do some marking to get movement information in the Chifungwe area," I said.

"My door is always open and I will be glad to help in any way that I can," he said. "But before you leave I want to give you something that will help you remember your experience in Zambia." Having said this, he reached in his desk drawer and pulled out a book with the title *Return to the Wild*. He autographed the book and wrote: *To David Patton, hoping this will recall happy memories of your visits to Luangwa Valley.*

"Thank you very much, Norman. This book will have a place of honor in my home when I return to the U.S.," I said as I shook his hand and then left the safari office and headed home.

The next morning when I went to the office Stan Stenton was back from making his rounds of the Luambe, Lukusuzi, and Nsefu Reserves on the east bank of the Luangwa. I had been told by CGO that Johnny Uys was going on home leave in about a month and Stenton would take Johnny's position as warden. For all practical purposes I was to start working with Stan as my official Game Department contact. When Johnny returned he would have a new assignment as park development officer and be stationed in Chilanga. When I walked into Stenton's room he was talking to his Game Guard Sergeant Nelson, who was getting ready to review his scouts that were heading for the bush.

"Do you want to walk through the review with me so that these scouts will know who you are?" Stan asked.

As a former military police sergeant I had been through this type of formation many times, but I thought this certainly would be a different review and it could also be informative and fun. Nelson called his Guards to attention, and Stan introduced me as a biologist assigned by the United Nations to work with the Game Department in the Luangwa Reserves and that they were to provide me assistance if needed when I was in their area. Stan walked in front and I followed about four steps behind as he looked at each man and his equipment on the first row and then proceeded to the second and last row. The main concern in this review was that each Guard had a working rifle with twenty rounds of ammunition and that their uniform and hat with a Game Department Badge were in good repair. The uniforms were well worn but clean, as were their knee socks and ankle-high shoes. Their rifles were old but it was obvious that they had been properly maintained. These

Guards were trained in a military fashion and responded appropriately when commands were given. Everything seemed to be in order, so Stan told Nelson to dismiss the ranks.

We returned to Stan's office, and I asked him if he could provide a letter authorizing me access to the Game Reserves and authorization to drive a Game Department vehicle. He said that he would have the letter ready by tomorrow.

"Yesterday I spent some time with Norman Carr discussing the Luangwa Survey, and I also need to talk to you about the same subject. Could we do that tomorrow?" I asked Stan.

"Any time tomorrow will be fine since I will be here all day," he said. "Maybe we can go to the Colonial Club and talk while having a beer. You do drink beer, don't you?"

"Of course, but probably not as much as the expatriates here do," I replied.

After my visit with Norman I spent time looking at the aerial photographs of the Chifungwe Plain and surrounding area, particularly road and vehicle tracks made through the bush as compared to 1960. There was definite evidence that vehicle use had increased over the past five years. The road from Mpika over the escarpment to the Valley was more defined than the section coming through the Munyamadzi Corridor from the South Reserve. The question was: Why is the road being used more now than in the past? This was a question that I would ask Stan Stenton.

The next day I was busy looking at the set of aerial photos I had brought with me from Chilanga when Stan walked in.

"Are you ready for a beer?" he asked.

After looking at him for a second I realized that he probably needed the beer more than I did and he just seemed like he wanted to talk. We were early at the Colonial Club and had the main room to ourselves since it was not time for the heavy drinkers to arrive.

"You look like you had a bad morning," I said to Stan.

"Well I got called to Minister Mbewe's office this morning and asked why I was not hiring more Africans in administrative and senior positions."

"And what did you say to him?" I asked.

"I tried to explain that most of the senior and administrative positions require a certain educational level for the job, and in Fort Jameson we did not have qualified Africans. Although we could probably find them in Lusaka and bring them north, I would rather use local people as much as I can," Stan explained.

Mbewe was appointed Minister of the Eastern Province by President Kaunda. These ministerial jobs were given to people who were active in UNIP (United National Independence Party), and during the move to independence many Africans were promised jobs that were now being held by the whites. As the Minister of the Province, Mbewe had to respond to the local UNIP party and try to address their complaints—one of which was employment.

"Mbewe seemed to understand the situation and asked that I try to employ more Africans, even in less important jobs, and that he would support a budget request from the Game Department for that purpose," Stan said.

"We probably could hire several office boys for errand work, but I will not be in too much of a hurry to do this so that I am not seen as just responding to a politician. But, lets change the subject; we did not come here to talk about my problems but about yours and the Luangwa Survey," he said.

"One of the items I wanted to ask you about is the marking crew and how it functions in the Department," I said.

"Basically what we have are two crews that use capture guns, but one is for cropping and the other is marking elephants to try to determine their daily and seasonal movements. Both crews work independently but members can switch between crews when necessary. Each crew has a leader who is responsible for the capture gun and drugs, one member always has a .375 rifle for safety, and the other serves as an assistant. The crew leader is responsible for selecting an animal for marking.

"Right now the focus is on solitary non-adolescent males that are in the range of fifteen years or older. During adolescence, cows will drive off these young males that are twelve to thirteen years old, and they join a bachelor group. These males travel great distances during the rainy season when food is plentiful, and their movements will provide good information on what areas they use inside and outside the reserves.

"Our efforts are limited to the South Reserve because of the cost of having to be on an expedition of several days to distant areas of the Valley and require a lot of travel time," Stan explained.

"What is the marking procedure?" I asked.

"It is fairly simple. Once an elephant is down, we record several body measurements, check for scars that can be used as identifiers, and then paint an identification number on each side and in both ears. The paint used has a rubber base and lasts about three weeks in the best of circumstances.

"With the number of people we have moving in and out of the reserve, we are starting to get some good movement information. All visitors and employees are required to report sightings of marked animals and indicate their location on a map that I keep in our radio room," Stan said.

"We certainly need a better way of marking elephants than using rubberized paint. In some cases we mark the animal with a white number and the next day it is all covered with mud or scrapped off against a tree."

"When would be a good time for me to go out with the marking crew just to observe?" I asked.

"The crew goes out two or three times a month. Because we have a heavy work schedule for other management activities I cannot let the crew work full time marking but have to assign them other duties as well. From the schedule now posted it looks like you can go with them in about two weeks."

"That is fine with me because I have more aerial photos to scan, and next week I plan to be at Mfuwe to go in the field with Johnny Uys," I said. "When I arrived at Fort Jameson Airport I took a notice off of the bulletin board advertising a Cessna 170 for rent by Robert Lawson. Do you know Lawson?" I asked.

"He is one of our contract pilots and flies out of Mpika," Stan said.

"So he is someone that you trust and can recommend to me as a good pilot? Because I may need to use him and his plane to do some aerial census work."

Stan agreed and stated that the CGO said that he had sufficient funds allocated to our project so that I could do a lot of flying either for reconnaissance, census work, or for emergency purposes.

"Lawson listed a telephone number; can you actually get a call through to Mpika?" I asked.

"Making a call to that town is just about the same as making a call to Lusaka; you give the operator the number and then wait. It may take several hours if the lines are busy with government business, but if you are lucky it may only take an hour. All you can do is try.

"Have Yvonne place the call the first thing in the morning and you may get through," Stan said.

Another topic I wanted to discuss was help from the Game Department when we moved to our office after construction was finished. It was about a mile outside of town. We would need a night guard, an office assistant, and a Game Guard to go with me on expeditions in the Valley. Stan suggested that I consider Joshua Njovo, one of his young Game Guards, to help around the office and as a general go-for for whatever we wanted. He said that later he would assign one of the marking crew Guards as our scout and guide, and I could use him whenever needed, but he would like him to continue doing his regular duties until I had a specific trip to make.

"If you like I will have Joshua report to you tomorrow to discuss the possibility of him working for you.

"My only concern about Joshua is that he takes time to attend all the UNIP meetings and has a strong opinion about blacks replacing whites in their current jobs. He has been through our basic Game Guard training and appears to be an okay employee, but you will just have to put him to work to see how he does," Stan said.

While we were talking I saw a gentleman headed toward our table who reminded me of the movie actor Stuart Granger, a tall thin man with white hair who had made films in Africa in the 1940s. He sat down at our table and interrupted our conversation without an invitation and started complaining to Stan that cropping elephants was wrong because it was taking animals that could be killed by hunters who were his clients. He never did introduce himself, but Stan introduced him to me as Ian Finch, a well-known guide and long-time resident of Zambia.

Ian was born in Livingston but got his education in England and worked for the colonial government in the transportation and roads department until the mid fifties when he left government service and started his own business as a hunting guide. Ian catered to the very rich and sometimes famous people and had friends in high government positions. Despite having these connections to officials, he was openly critical of the black government and stated quite frankly that no blacks should be allowed to hunt in the game management areas that had been established with colonial funds.

He already knew who I was and criticized the "ridiculous idea of counting animals from an airplane when guides like me could provide the information on elephant numbers." He flatly stated, "There are six thousand elephants in the Luangwa Valley, and none of the meat from the cropping station should go to villagers living in the corridor." Stan later said he fancied himself as an expert on all matters of wildlife and would show up at meetings in Lusaka and Fort Jameson any time the cropping scheme or the game management areas were being discussed. The Game Department never could find out where he was getting his information about activities and events happening in the Valley, but it had to be from someone in the government.

Ian must have come to the conclusion that we were not about to get into an argument in the Colonial Club were he was surrounded by friends because he got up and left in about the same manner as he had arrived.

"You should be aware that some people openly oppose what the Game Department is doing in trying to control animal populations by cropping. Opposition comes from several sources: expatriates working for the government and white settlers who stayed in the country following independence," Stan said.

"Since the Luangwa Survey includes determining animal populations their opposition will be extended to the FAO project. Fortunately these people are low in number and are not considered a significant force in getting their views accepted.

"Let's have one more Castle beer, and by then I will be ready to call it a day," Stan said.

"I'll buy," I said.

The next morning I had Yvonne place the call to Robert Lawson at the number he listed for Mpika. The operator tried several times and finally told Yvonne that the lines were too busy with government calls but that she would try every half hour if someone would be available to take the call if it went through.

"I'll be here most of the morning, so tell the operator to keep trying," I said.

Just as I got through talking to Yvonne, Joshua Njovo came out of Stan's office and said, "I would like to talk to you about working on the Luangwa project. Senior Game Ranger Stenton told me about the project that you are starting and that you need an office boy to help with errands, checking mail, daytime security, etc., and I would like to do this to learn new things for future employment," he said.

"Tell me about yourself." I requested.

"I was six years old when my uncle took me to the Catholic church at Fort Jameson. He left me with the Sisters and asked if they could take care of me. He told them that I did not have a father, that my mother had just died of malaria, and that he could not take care of me because he had no money. My uncle did not have employment and was on his way to the copper belt to see if he could get a job in the mines. He promised the Sisters that he would return in a few weeks and take me to live with him in Ndola. Several weeks passed and the Sisters never heard from my uncle. I had no place to go, so they kept me with their other orphaned children. My uncle returned several years ago, and I now live with him in my old village.

"When I turned sixteen I was hired by the Game Department to wash vehicles, do errands and odd jobs, and train to be a Game Guard. I have been working for the Department for two years," he explained. As he talked, I was evaluating his language skills, behavior, sincerity, and appearance. He was clean and neat. He was easy to understand, and it was obvious that his years at the orphanage had a strong influence on his command of the new language. While I was concentrating on observing his demeanor and expressions as he talked, Yvonne came into the room, "Robert Lawson is on the telephone; can you take his call now?" she asked.

"I can take the call here in my room.

"Hello, is this Robert Lawson?" I asked.

"Yes it is, and you must be David Patton," he responded.

"Owen Rhodes told me that I have funds for aerial surveys in the Luangwa Valley, and Stan Stenton says that you do contract work for the Game Department."

"That is correct, and my plane is located here at Mpika. What do you have in mind?"

"I will be doing reconnaissance flights and aerial counts of elephant and buffalo as part of the Luangwa Survey, and I will need your help—or maybe you could rent me the plane to use. Now that I know you are available I will make some plans and get back to you in several weeks. Is the telephone number that we have the best number to use?"

"The telephone number is a good one, and there will always be someone to answer the phone even if I am not home. Thanks for thinking of me, and I will be glad to work with you on the projects that you have indicated," Robert said.

With that we said goodbye and hung up.

"Now Joshua, back to our discussion. Yes, I do need an office boy, and Stan has recommended you for the job.

"You do not need to start right now, but our office building should be ready in about two weeks, and that would be a good time for you to go on our payroll. Also at about that time I expect the other member of the survey team to arrive, and between the two of us we should keep you busy.

"I will keep in touch and let you know if anything changes that might affect the starting date."

Joshua left the office and seemed quite happy that he might soon have a job with our survey crew, but I had this uneasy feeling that his interests might include something more than he had been willing to tell me.

Chapter Six

The following week I received a radio message from CGO that he would be flying to Mfuwe on Thursday with Johnny Uys and I could meet them for an aerial reconnaissance over the Luangwa Valley. After my discussions with Norman, Stan, and Owen, I was looking forward to making the flight. By now I knew the locations of the main topographic and cultural features including the Muchinga escarpment, the Luangwa River, the reserve headquarters, the Mpika road, and the Chifungwe Plain.

During the time I had been in Fort Jameson my transportation was rather iffy. Sometimes a Game Department vehicle was available, but most of the time I had to either walk or make arrangements for a driver to pick me up and take me to the office. FAO had ordered two Toyota Land Cruisers from Japan, but they were still on the boat headed for Beira, Mozambique, then by rail to a freight company in Blantyre, Malawi, that was supposed to deliver them prepaid to Fort Jameson. As I found out later, it would be up to me to get them to Zambia from Malawi.

During the regular radio call to CGO I asked if he could send a vehicle from Chilanga for me to use until the Toyotas arrived. He said that they did have a vehicle as a loaner and would have a driver bring it to Fort Jameson, but it could not be delivered for another week. In the meantime I asked Stan if something was available for a week until the Land Rover arrived. He provided me with an open vehicle with a canvas top called a Mini-mote. It was only twenty-horse power but was adequate for my purposes.

I caught a regularly scheduled Game Department Land Rover that was going to Mfuwe early Thursday morning to be there when CGO arrived from Lusaka. The ride to Mfuwe was interesting, as this was my first road trip through the rural areas. Along the way we encountered many small villages, a variety of animals, and lots of brush fires. I asked the Game Guard driver, "Why are there so many fires this time of year?"

"Local people set fires to clear areas for planting crops," he responded. "They also use fire to get small animals to move away from the heat while the people wait to kill them for food. This is an old practice that I have seen used since I was a little boy in a village," he said.

It took about ninety minutes to reach Mfuwe over the dirt road with its red dust, but I was glad to have time to familiarize myself with the surrounding countryside between Fort Jameson and Mfuwe. This was a road that I would travel many times by myself, and I wanted to know where the danger points might be and the distance between villages. The CGO arrived in the four-seat Cherokee, which was good for point-to-point travel but was not the best for reconnaissance work because it was a low wing aircraft. In this plane the wings blocked the view under the plane, and the only way to see the area was to bank right and left. With Johnny Uys as our pilot, we took off from the dirt runway and climbed to 1000 feet.

The Luangwa Valley is a linear depression some sixty miles wide and four hundred miles long extending from Fort Hill near the Malawi border to Feira on the Zambezi River. Its watershed area contains approximately 56,200 square miles. The area of primary interest for our survey included only that portion of the watershed from the lower end of the South Reserve northward and contains approximately 31,300 square miles.

The Luangwa River roughly divides the Valley in half. Its headwaters are located near the Malawi border and flows in a southwesterly direction for four hundred and fifty miles to the Zambezi. Three hundred and eleven miles of the Luangwa were in our survey area. The river itself is geologically old, characterized by oxbows, lagoons, and a wide alluvial flood plain. The Valley is part of the East African Rift system and was formed by the sinking of land between two parallel faults. The well-defined depression makes the Valley an ecological unit, with soil, vegetation, and animal life differing considerably from that found on the surrounding plateau. This was October, and the vegetation was dry and produced a light brownish color.

"In a few minutes when we get over the Chifungwe Plain you will be seeing more elephants than one would think possible in such a small area," Owen said.

Johnny made a slow bank, tilting the plane for us to get a view, and we could see numerous herds of elephants in groups of five to more than twenty-five. There were several large herds of buffalo that took off in a trot when Johnny went lower. One herd contained at least two hundred animals. As

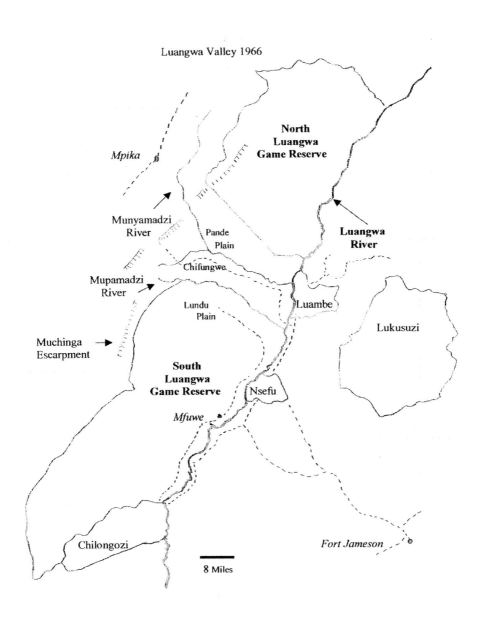

they moved over the dry plain, dust rose and drifted south in the slight breeze. Several solitary elephant bulls were present and turned toward the noise of the plane, pushed their ears forward, and raised their heads.

"Any time you fly low over an elephant the reaction is almost always the same, they stop, flap their ears forward, and throw their head and trunk upward," Johnny said.

We flew north to the North Reserve, and the density of tree vegetation increased noticeably after crossing over the plains. We turned 180 degrees to cross back into the South Reserve into the mopane vegetation. Mopane trees are sometimes known as the butterfly tree because the shape of the leaves, when open, look like butterfly wings. The leaves turn yellow and red in September and October and are sources of food for many mammal species, including tree squirrels and elephants. The Mupamadzi and Munyamadzi rivers only had a trickle of water in some places. At low altitude we could easily see elephant damage to tree limbs to the extent that there was a definite browse line at about twenty feet matching the height to which an elephant can reach. This browse line was what Norman Carr had told me about earlier. We flew over the end of the South Reserve, and Johnny banked to follow the meandering Luangwa River to Mfuwe.

We gained altitude to take a look at the river and the effects of meandering which creates the oxbow lakes and lagoons. The Luangwa is a miniature Mississippi and almost as powerful when at high water. *It is a magnificent river with water actions tearing down one area while building up another,* I thought to myself.

It was easy to see where new lagoons were ready to form when the river would cut through the bank and straighten out, leaving an isolated pool. Other areas where lagoons were filling in and new growth beginning from the rich soil were just as prominent. Many lagoons had lush aquatic vegetation and lots of hippos. As we flew along the river I made notes of places that I would need to see from the ground to get a feel for vegetation productivity and animal effects on vegetation.

As the plane turned into the final approach to land, I began to realize that the survival and diversity of wildlife in the Valley was dependent on two ecological factors: the elephant and the river. Both have a great potential to affect soil and vegetation. If either were out of balance in the watershed, then other animals, including people, would be affected. After seeing the elephants from the air and their reaction to the plane I began to get an idea for marking that I would pursue, but I wanted to wait until I saw elephants in the bush. Johnny lined the Cherokee up with the runway, lowered the flaps to slow down and the runway came up to meet us. We taxied toward the end to turn around, and abruptly Johnny shut off the engine.

Off to the right of the plane at the edge between the grass and dirt was a mother cheetah looking at us with blood dripping from her mouth. In front of her was a small impala and her two juvenile cubs getting their meal for the day. The mother did not seem too alarmed but did not take her eyes off the plane while the cubs got their fill. We watched them for about fifteen minutes, and then the mother decided it was time to leave and all three walked deeper into the grass and scattered shrubs and trees. Johnny restarted the plane and we taxied to the loading area.

We remained at Mfuwe just long enough for CGO and Johnny to give instructions to several Department employees, and then we took off and headed for Fort Jameson. It was a short flight and I was met at the terminal by Stan.

"I will be coming back next week by road and will be driving a Land Rover for you to use until the Toyotas arrive," Johnny said and then he and CGO took off for Lusaka.

Stan and I left the airport, and on the way to town I briefed him on the flight and our discussions. I told him that I recognized all the major landmarks because I had seen them in stereo on the aerial photographs.

"I have seen the photos as a flat picture but I have never seen them through the stereoscope. Would you show me how to do this the next time you are working with the prints?" he asked.

"Of course, and there is something in the photographs that I have never seen before that I would like to ask you about," I said.

The following week Johnny brought the Land Rover to Fort Jameson, and I took him to Mfuwe where he stayed in a house that he called the "mushroom" because that is exactly what it looked like. It was a two-story building with the second story containing the guest bedroom. The draping thatch roof gave it the appearance that fit the name. There were plenty of windows in the mushroom, and air flowed through the building at night to make it a pleasant place to sleep. The mushroom was near an old oxbow lagoon, and it was not unusual to see elephant, impala, and scattered buffalo feeding and watering there in the evenings. There were lots of doves in the trees surrounding the lagoon, and their cooing seemed identical to the sound that mourning doves make around the world.

There was some time left before darkness arrived, and I decided to walk from the mushroom down a dirt road toward another house occupied by a Game ranger assigned to Mfuwe. On my way back I got about one hundred yards when a rhino came out of the brush and onto the road about twenty yards away. He turned and started walking toward me. I quickly looked around, and my only protection was a tree off to my right. I started side-stepping in that direction while at the same time looking directly ahead. It seemed strange that he did not appear to know that I was there or did not care. He kept coming toward me but not at the rate I would have expected had he felt I was a threat. When I had moved to the edge of the road and stepped off, I quickly ran behind the tree to get it between him and me.

At this point the rhino kept on walking on the road for another fifteen to twenty yards and went off into the brush. I was still waiting at the tree when about a half hour later Johnny's cook came down the road past the point where the rhino had gone off into the bush. I stepped out from behind the tree and told him that I was going back to the mushroom but I was confronted by a rhino that stepped out of the bush in front of me. The cook looked at me and with a big smile said, "You must have met our pet rhino, Chipembere. He stays around this area and is not a threat, so when he comes down the road just step off and let him go on by," he said. "Johnny must have forgotten to tell you about him."

I wondered what else Johnny had forgotten to tell me, or was this just his way to test my nerves? When I got back to the mushroom that evening I did not mention the encounter with the rhino to Johnny, but I am sure the cook told him about it later.

After breakfast the next morning we went for a drive to find elephants. It did not take long as the concentrations were scattered adjacent to the river and near lagoons. We passed many small solitary bulls, and there was no shortage of family groups of five to ten animals. I was so completely absorbed in watching these magnificent animals slowly move through the vegetation, I didn't say much to Johnny. We rounded a curve and there was a bull moving across the road about twenty yards in front of us. Johnny stopped the vehicle and got out.

"Get out slowly and walk around the back to this side and we will watch for a few minutes," Johnny said. "What we have here is a bull that weighs about four tons. With the ivory he is carrying and from his size, I would estimate that he is about twenty-five years old.

"The race of elephant we have in the Luangwa Valley is the bush elephant and differs from the forest elephant in tropical areas in that it is larger and the tusks are thicker, curve upward, and are softer, making it more easy to carve and therefore more valuable. Tusks of the forest elephant are long and narrow and harder.

"Let's wait until this bull gets out of the vegetation and into the opening off to our left, and then we will follow him a few yards. I know this bull, and I often see him here in this same area.

"Okay let's walk toward him but keep behind me and to the left. What I am going to do is try to get him to notice us and demonstrate with a charge, but it will not be a full charge and he will stop. Although he is uneasy, he will detect that we are not a threat. I want you to see the characteristics of the demonstration which is to let us know that he knows we are near and is disturbed. We will walk towards him and see what he does. If he turns toward us and starts to move rapidly in our direction, don't move unless I say, 'Run.' Then get the vehicle between you and him as fast as you can."

Intentionally we had only gone about fifteen yards from the vehicle. When we got to within twenty yards of the elephant, his trunk went into the air and he turned in our direction. As he started moving, his head went up and while shaking from side to side, flapping his ears, and making lots of noise by trumpeting, he then rushed forward a few yards and abruptly stopped. He stood there for a few seconds and then turned around and retreated across the road, his tail raised, and he was looking slightly backward at us as if he expected us to follow.

"Congratulations, you are still alive and have just survived your first elephant charge," Johnny said. "If that bull had meant business he would have dropped his head, laid his ears back, and come full force at us. I don't intend to get one to demonstrate a full charge to show the difference, so just remember what you saw. Also I told you to get behind the vehicle if he charged. The problem is that a bull of this size can get his tusks under the car and flip it over, but this would be a rare occurrence. However, you have to keep in mind that these bloody beasts are strong.

"In working with elephants there are two things that you must remember," Johnny said. "Stay away from cows with calves, and know where you are going by looking ahead and around you so that you don't inadvertently surprise an animal that you did not know was there."

We got back into the vehicle and drove for several miles and then stopped to watch a family group cross the road and travel into the brush to an opening several hundred yards away.

"A family group consists of a female and her offspring," Johnny said. "These groups range from several to over ten animals and is lead by a cow. Family groups can form together in a larger herd led by the oldest and probably the wisest cow among the group.

"This cow is the matriarch of the herd. Bulls generally live in small bachelor groups consisting of a few young males and an older bull," Johnny said. "Bulls will rejoin the herds when females are in heat. During times of danger, the cows circle around the younger members of the family group.

"What we will do now is to follow this family group in the brush just for a few minutes so you can get the smell of fresh sign from elephants," Johnny said.

We walked onto the trail for about twenty yards. The odor was something that does not compare to anything else. It was not heavy or disagreeable but had the scent of what I would call old mushrooms or mildew on clothing. The odor lingers longer with high humidity after a rain. It was an odor that I imagined related to the past and the time of twelve thousand years ago when large mammals roamed the earth. We returned to the vehicle and continued down the road until we came to an opening with trees that had been damaged by elephants. The trunks were four to six inches, but the height was only five to six feet. All of the branches had been broken off, and there were only a few green leaves scattered on the remaining branch stubs. The area of destruction was about fifteen acres and contained lots of elephant droppings and footprints.

The last item on Johnny's list was to look at an elephant exclosure that had been constructed to show the difference between trees outside compared to those inside. The exclosure was well built with ten-inch posts imbedded in concrete. The areas contrasted significantly. The outside looked much like the previous area, but the inside had undamaged trees in a higher density and lots more low woody vegetation and grass. Johnny said that this was where he brought guests when they said that elephants do not damage vegetation.

Since it was already past noon I told Johnny that I would buy him lunch at the lodge and then I had to head back to Fort Jameson. At lunch Johnny talked about his upcoming leave and his planned trip to the U.S. He was excited and asked for recommendations of parks, reserves, and other places to visit and persons to contact. I told him that I would make a list for both items within the next two weeks.

The trip back to Fort Jameson was the first time that I was alone in a vehicle driving in a rural area and on the left side of the road. It gave me a chance to practice and get used to the idea that I was not on the wrong side. Transition from right to left side driving is not difficult if one remembers that the driver's side is always in the middle of the road. I only passed a few vehicles coming the other way, so the trip was uneventful until I saw a Zambian policeman about fifty yards ahead standing on the left side of the road waving his arm. He was in full uniform, and, thinking that this was an emergency, I stopped and asked if I could help. He said that he had to get to Fort Jameson and needed a ride.

I said, "OK get in."

He asked that I wait a minute and he rushed away. In a few minutes he was back and had another five people with him.

"Who are these people?" I asked.

"They are my family that need to go to Fort Jameson with me," he said.

Before I could tell him no, they were all climbing into the rear two side seats with all of their belongings, including a sack of dried fish that smelled to high heaven. We were only about ten miles from Fort Jameson so I unzipped my window and the back window about halfway to let the air flow through. The trip from there was unpleasant but bearable, and it taught me a lesson about stopping to pick up a single person when there were probably several others hidden out of sight. Later I found out that this is a common way for families to catch a ride with Europeans.

Chapter Seven

I was working on a draft for background material for the report when Stan walked in.

"You said that you wanted to show me something on the aerial photographs," he said.

"Before showing you the spot, I need to get you oriented on how to use two photographs to view them in three dimensions. Basically aerial photographs are taken along a straight line, and each photograph overlaps one with the other. The amount of overlap is about one-third of the photograph so that you get the same object on two photographs. The idea is to photograph the same spot from a slightly different angle, and this is achieved because the plane is moving away from the last point the photo was made. Place one photograph under the left lens and the overlapping photo under the right lens. The center of each lens should be over the center of the photograph. Now look through the stereoscope. What do you see?" I asked.

"I can see the objects, but they are fuzzy."

"Look at the Mushroom at Mwfue, and move the right photo slightly back and forth, up and down until you get a sharp image."

"There it is; I can see the height of buildings," Stan said.

"Now that you know how to see in three dimensions, I want you to look at these next two photographs. Center the photographs on the circular area that I point to with my pencil when you have 3-D. Okay now what is the object that I am pointing to?" I asked.

Stan slowly lifted his head and said, "Yes, I know what it is, but you are not supposed to know that it exists. Only a few people in the government know about this geological structure, and it is not shown on any public maps. I am surprised that these photographs have not been confiscated, but the photo survey company was probably never told about avoiding this area of the South Reserve. However, since you will be working in the area and may run across it in the field, I will only tell you that it is a formation that could contain diamonds. The government believes that it has great potential for the economy of the country, but its development would mean destruction of a large area of prime wildlife habitat for many species. It is currently under lease for potential mining to a corporation in South Africa.

"Now that you know what it is, just keep the information to yourself and let's go on to another subject," he suggested.

I thought to myself that this subject was very sensitive, and it would be best not to go near the formation when I was roaming through the South Reserve.

"I have an idea about marking elephants, and I need to go out with the marking crew to see them go through the process," I said to Stan. "I have considerable experience in using the capture gun in immobilizing deer in the U.S., and I want to see how the techniques I have used differ from what you are using on elephants," I informed him.

"One thing I would like you to do while you are with the marking crew is to observe their actions to see if you can determine what is happening to the M99 drug," Stan said. "We have to account for every drop of liquid, and so far we are not doing so well. I just need to find out what is going on. It may be our methods, but it could be that some of it is being siphoned off for other purposes and disappearing.

"The cost of M99 is increasing and getting harder to get in South Africa because of the embargo that is now in effect, so we need to explore other sources of supply. Right now I think that we have only enough drug to mark about five to six animals," Stan said.

"I'll watch the marking crew closely to see how the drug is drawn from the supply bottle and how it is transferred to the capture dart," I said to Stan. "One other thing that I need to do is get to the cropping station to look at a few elephants to see their physical characteristics up close. I can do this at the abattoir on a day when they have brought in some recently killed animals.

"Sometime today I need to go into town to see if I can find leather crafting tools. Do you have any suggestions where I might find such things?" I asked.

"You might try I.S. Jasat Store; he seems to have a lot of small tools and just might have what you need. I know that there are several leather workers who are buying skins from the abattoir, and they must get their tools from one of the Indian shops," he said.

The Indian shops were concentrated in a separate section of the town from the other stores. All of them were located on a one-way dirt road that made a loop around the shops in an oval pattern. Indian shops were a controversial issue and were always under scrutiny by UNIP. These shops only had a token number of African workers, and the shops were run by family members of the Indian owners. I noticed that almost all of the shops had a sign that read: CASH 10% DISCOUNT. Many African customers could not pay cash, and the store owners had charge accounts carried over month to month. Because the locals could not pay cash, they never received a discount no matter how much they purchased.

When I entered the Jasat store, the owner himself greeted me. The word had gotten around that there was now a family of Americans living in Fort Jameson, and it appeared that the news traveled from shop to shop as I went to each one around the oval. Jasat introduced himself as the owner and immediately offered me a 20 percent discount on anything I bought today or in the future. His store had a lot of dry goods that were mostly purchased by expatriates. He also had considerable canned goods of fruit, beans, etc., that he imported from England, the Netherlands, and South Africa. I asked if he had leather punches and whether he had different hole sizes.

"I had a special request from a person that works at the cropping station to order two punches about three months ago, but he never returned to pick them up even though they are paid for," Jasat said. "I will sell them to you for half price. If the owner returns I will refund his purchase price and you can pay me the other half. If he does not return then you have purchased a bargain."

The two punches were exactly what I needed, one made a one-fourth-inch hole and the other one was a three-eighths-inch size. I thanked him for the discount and left the store. This was just one of many purchases that I made at the I.S. Jasat store over the next twelve months. The more I bought there the more I learned of his business practices which really discriminated against the locals. I also heard a story about Jasat that I did not believe at first, but as time went on I thought that it might have been true. The story was that several years ago, before Independence, there was severe competition between Jasat and another Indian shop owner. His competitor did not show up for work one day and was found dead in his Land Rover behind his shop, shot through the head. The police were never able to connect Jasat to the murder, but rumors through the expatriates were that he had hired an assassin to get rid of the competition.

I left the store with my leather punches in addition to a small hammer and a copper soldering iron. The next item that I needed was a solid block of wood about 4x4x2 inches, and I found this at a small lumber shop that milled their own wood for local construction. With these items available I was now ready to start the first phase of my special project.

My scheduled trip to go out with the marking crew had been delayed because of changes in personnel assignments, but the day finally arrived. I left Fort Jameson in time to get to Mfuwe by 8:00 A.M. to meet the crew. The leader was Ian Botha, a young man of about twenty-four who had been educated in South Africa where he gained his wildlife experience in Kruger

National Park. Ian was an easy-going individual who seemed to get along well with Africans and Europeans alike. He was not particularly fond of some of the U.K. expatriates and had made plans to go to the U.S. to work on a degree in wildlife management. His two assistants, Sam Mlenga and James Ngulwe, both had Game Guard status and were assigned to the marking crew to get training and experience in working with live animals. Sam was a few years older than James and was not afraid to take charge when the situation was appropriate. James was a little more reserved but was very knowledgeable about the bush, and I only had to ask questions for him to respond.

Ian was responsible for the capture equipment, including the drugs, and James was primarily a driver with Sam the gun bearer. Both switched duties every other day, and Ian was training them in the use of the capture equipment. The intent was that some time over the next few years they would be the ones replacing the white expatriates and doing the marking. My trip to Mfuwe was pleasant because in the early morning hours there is very little traffic on the road to the South Reserve. Along the route there was a major vegetation change from a type of brachystegia woodlands at 4,000 feet to 2,000 feet with savannah and mopane intermixed. The number of birds and small mammals was more than one could learn by just traveling the road, but seeing them fly over or scurrying across in front of the vehicle was always worth the trip. Haze from smoldering fires often lingered in the lower depressions, and, except for the road and vehicles, the factors that created this condition probably have not changed for thousands of years. Local people had discovered the use of fire and still use it as in the past. The burned vegetation did provide nutrients to improve crop production, and the heat assisted their hunting of small mammals.

One of the things that I had to do to get to Mfuwe was to cross the Luangwa River. When I arrived at the river's edge the pontoon was there, ready for business. The pontoon, as it was called, consisted of empty oil drums tied together with steel cable. It had a wooden top made similar to a box top with sides that extended down over the drums. Each end of the pontoon had a let-down flap that allowed two vehicles to drive over the flap to park on the floor and exit the other side. The pontoon was secured to two steel cables extending across the river. One was overhead and connected to pulleys on steel upright posts; the other was on waist-high steel rails with pulleys and was used to pull the pontoon across the river. Three men using wooden handles with a notch that slipped over the cable provided power. By scooting the handle forward and then pulling backward in unison the three men could easily pull the pontoon across the river.

On the other side the flap was lowered to the bank and the vehicles could drive off. At the river crossing where the pontoon was located there was a deep pool that was a favorite place for a large number of hippos and crocodiles. The hippos were always noisily making their grunting sound and had an occasional fight that kept the water stirred up and muddy. The crocs stayed along the banks waiting for their next meal. I had the thought, when crossing the river, of what would happen if the pontoon tipped over with vehicles and passengers. The chances of survival in the hippo- and croc-infested water were not very good.

When we arrived at the other side I drove off and headed for the lodge to meet the marking crew. Ian was waiting, and we lost no time in getting headed out to the bush. The goal for today was to mark at least one young bachelor bull, and the crew had already selected an area about an hour's drive north of the lodge to search for the right animal. They had been to this same area several times and knew it was a place where there were single bulls and several young bachelor groups hanging out. When we arrived at the general area, Ian stopped to get the capture gun ready. The drugs were kept in a locked steel box and were under his control at all times.

This was Sam's day to carry the .375 H & H magnum. James would work directly with Ian once the elephant was down. I asked Sam which caliber of rifle he preferred for elephants.

"When I was on elephant control I used a .375 rifle all the time and never had a problem. However, I always took a heart or lung shot and never fired at one coming full charge where I would have had to hit the brain because this is tricky," Sam said.

I noticed that Ian was just getting the glass syringe ready to insert into the bottle that had a rubber top. He pulled the plunger out about an inch and a half and inserted the needle into the rubber cap, pushed the plunger in to create pressure inside the bottle, and then pulled the plunger out again to draw the drug into the glass syringe. As he pulled the needle out of the cap there were several drops of the drug that came out with it, and this explained Stan's problem of accounting for the drug.

"Ian," I said, "Let me show you a technique that I learned from a nurse several years ago when using drugs to immobilize deer. Because drugs are expensive and dangerous the Department needs to account for every drop used or wasted. There is a simple way to draw liquid from a rubber-capped bottle and not lose any fluid. You will notice that when you pulled the syringe out of the bottle there were several drops that also came out with the needle and fell to the ground.

"Before inserting the needle into the bottle, pull the plunger out just the same amount that you want of the drug and then insert the needle up through the rubber cap and inject air. With the bottle turned upside down and with the needle tip below the fluid level, slowly pull the plunger out until you have the correct amount of fluid in the glass syringe. Then pull the needle from the bottle.

"Because you injected the same amount of air as the liquid you removed there is no excess pressure to push out liquid when you remove the needle. Give this technique a try the next time you fill a syringe," I suggested.

With the capture gun loaded, we got back into the vehicle, and James started slowly down the road. All four of us were looking left and right into openings and edges to see if we could find a suitable animal. We passed several large, old, mature bulls accompanied by young ones that probably were recently run off from a family group by the matriarch cow.

While looking for elephants I was also noting the diversity of animal species that existed in this area and contribute to the overall scheme of life in the valley. Impalas were running and jumping trying to get across the road in front of us; baboons and their young looked up for a few seconds as we passed and then went back to picking up items from the ground. Waterbuck, puku, and zebra were scattered on both sides of the road, and the ever-present vervet monkeys were trying to steal food from each other. But one of the most enjoyable sights was the stately baobab tree with its twisted branches and thick trunk giving the appearance of a short, fat person with unmanaged hair. It is a tree of many uses. Fresh leaves are used as a vegetable, the coating around the edible seed has a refreshing tart taste, and bark fiber is good for ropes and baskets. While baobabs are widely distributed in the lower elevations in the reserve, it is disappearing because of its preference as a food item by elephants. An elephant can insert its two tusks into the tree just under the bark and pull upward to strip off long pieces. For every standing baobab we saw that still had some bark, there were three or four others that were whittled down to stump level with nothing left but remnant pieces of woody material.

After about an hour of searching, James pointed out two bulls, a young one that matched our age and size criteria along with a bull that probably was another eight to ten years older. Both were feeding along together at a slow pace and they were just about one hundred yards from the road. James starting maneuvering the vehicle slowly off the road, staying within the trees until we got to within about fifty yards of them.

We got out of the vehicle, and Ian, Sam, and I started walking easily toward the two bulls. James and Sam were both looking over the terrain to see if other dangerous animals might be near our two elephants while Ian and I kept our attention directed to the two feeding animals. We were downwind and enough to the left for a good rump shot. The older bull was another twenty yards in front of the younger one and was a little more in the open. Ian kept trees between him and the young bull until we got to within twenty yards. This would have been a perfect shot for a safari hunter with a .375, but we were about to hit this bull with a dart instead of a bullet.

Our main concern was with the other bull and what he would do. Ian took aim for the rump and pulled the trigger. The *poof* from the gun must not have been heard by either bull. The young one flinched forward a few feet. The dart had penetrated the skin and remained attached. The needle on the capture dart has a small barb that is just large enough to hold the dart in place but not large enough to cause damage or make it difficult to remove. The older bull looked backward with his trunk in the air, but we were still on the downwind side and were not detected. The younger bull turned back around and returned to feeding. All we could do was wait. No one talked or moved from behind the trees.

The young bull started to weave a little at fifteen minutes and went down in twenty. The older bull immediately turned and rushed to his side trying to get him to rise. He struggled several times with his trunk and tusks, but the young bull was now completely out and made no attempt to get up. The older bull keep trying for another fifteen minutes and finally moved slowly away with an occasional glance back where the young bull lay. We were still behind the trees and starting to feel the anxiety from standing still so long.

When the older bull had moved off to a safe distance we left our tree protection and walked slowly up behind the immobilized animal. I put a small cloth over his left eye as he was laying on his right side. All the time Ian and I were working on the bull Sam was out in front of us scanning the area and with his .375 rifle at the ready position—just in case the other bull or any other dangerous animal decided to come our way. James had brought the vehicle up to our location, left the engine running, the doors open, and started helping Ian with the measurements while I painted a white number 15 on it sides and back. This was my first experience of laying my hands on a real live African elephant. The odor of the animal was just the same as when Johnny Uys and I were walking in the bush on a fresh trail. The pads on the bottom of the feet were made for travel over rough terrain, but at the same time they would mask any sound coming from this animal if he did not want something to hear him.

I looked at his left ear to see the thickness at the area where the ear has a depression that included the ear hole. The total concave area measured about twelve inches and was perfect for placing an ear tag of eight to ten inches. Although I did not mention this to Ian, Sam, or James, I was studying the elephant's body features and making notes. The thickness of the ear in the center of the concave was around one inch and made up mostly of gristle between two layers of skin. Blood flowed through several large veins and many small ones going out to the edge of the ear. There is good reason to call the elephant ear an air cooling unit. It took about forty minutes to complete the required measurements and to paint the number on his side and back.

With everything done, James loaded the equipment back into the vehicle. Sam and I got in the back, and Ian injected the antidote into a large vein in the ear. The M285 is fast acting, and Ian jumped into the Land Rover, and we drove off about twenty yards. The young bull started trying to raise himself by sort of rolling off to the left. On the third try he was up on his knees and finally stood fully upright. He was a little wobbly at first but started walking in the direction that the older bull had taken. We moved the vehicle back to the road and watched the young bull through the binoculars until he was out of sight. Having assured ourselves that the young bull was okay, we headed back to Mfuwe and the lodge for a beer.

I only stayed at the lodge for about an hour before leaving for Fort Jameson. As I went across the Luangwa on the pontoon, I got out of the vehicle to talk to some of the pontoon's power source. These young men were eager to talk as they pulled us across the water.

"Where are you from?" one asked. "You are not from the U.K. or South Africa."

"No," I said, "I am from the State of Arizona in the U.S., and I am in Zambia working with the Game and Fish Department."

"So we will see you again on our pontoon?" one said.

"Maybe you will tell us more about your job," the youngest of the three said.

"I certainly will be glad to talk to you any time we cross the Luangwa. Your job is important because if the pontoon was not here I could not do my work for the Game Department."

This statement evoked a smile from all three power men, and I suspect no one had ever told them that they and their jobs were important. One of the things that I had been told by the Jacobses in Rome, who were returning from Zambia, was that little gifts to local people that we worked with would create a lot of good will. I had brought many ball-point pens and books of matches with me from the U.S., so I took three pens from my briefcase and gave one to each man. We arrived on the east bank, the flap was lowered, and I drove off while waving goodbye to the power team.

The day was now slowly beginning to wind down, and I was glad to be going back to Fort Jameson. It was about 4:00 P.M., and animals were starting to show up again along the road edges. There was still considerable smoke in the air, and several new fires had been started that I had not seen in the morning. I had just gone through one village and was going past the last hut when I saw an old man standing at the side of the road looking into a recently started fire. I decided to stop just to see what he was doing but wondered if he could speak English. I pulled off the road, stopped the engine, and got out.

"Hello," he said without me saying a word. His English was very good, and I asked him where he learned the language.

"I used to work as a paper clerk for the colonial government before Independence, but now I do not have a job because it was eliminated by the new government," he said.

"Many of the people living in the village back there worked for the government but now they just try to grow some crops.

"It is difficult here, so close to the Game Reserve, because elephants and other animals leave the reserve at night and raid our gardens." While he was talking he noticed the Luangwa Command Insignia with its large elephant head on the side of my vehicle. "Maybe you can get the game people to kill some of these animals that destroy our crops," he said.

"I'll pass on your concern and request to the warden when I get back to town. But I have a question for you. When I came through this morning there were not as many fires as there are now. Who started these fires and for what purpose?" I asked. For a few seconds he stared at me and then pointed his finger upward to a jet plane with a con trail.

"It is people smoking in those planes and then throwing their lighted cigarettes out the windows," he said in a rather frank tone of voice. All I could think of was that if he believed that is how these fires are started then it is so intuitive to him that nothing I say will change his mind. However, I think that he knew what started these fires and why. He did have a slight grin on his face as though to say "ask a silly question and you will get a silly answer." I decided it was time to be on my way again. I thanked him for sharing the information and handed him several books of matches from my briefcase and said, "You might have some use for these." His smile turned into a large grin. I got back into my Land Rover and went on down the dusty road back to Fort Jameson.

Chapter Eight

After going out with the marking crew I decided that it was not necessary for me to go to the cropping station to look at more elephant ears. After all, how much difference can there be in the shape and general size of an ear from one elephant to another in the same age and size class that we wanted to mark? I had already resolved the questions I had about a better marking procedure, and it was now time to put my special project into action. I wanted to create an ear tag that would be permanent, require only one marking per animal, and be visible from the air so we could see it when we did the aerial surveys. I had everything ready except the ear tag and permission from the Game Department to try several tags on an experimental basis. I drove to the Game Department's office to talk with Stan about the idea of putting a round disk in an elephant's ear to replace marking an animal with paint.

I explained that there was at least three ways to mark an elephant: put a large numbered ear tag in the ear, a numbered collar around its neck, or use paint as is now being done. Each has its own advantages and disadvantages. The collar is possible and would last a long time. It could have a radio for tracking the animal's movements on foot or in the air. The collar and radio would be expensive and take several months to get ready. The collar itself was not a problem because equipment belts made of conveyor belt rubber were available commercially. A radio could be either purchased or made from electronic components also commercially available. Marking with paint was cheap, but the disadvantage of having a very short life made it ineffective. So for now, the ear tag seemed the best alternative.

"I think the idea sounds good, but where in the world would you get a tag that will meet your specifications?" Stan asked.

"I have already checked the telephone book for plastic manufacturers, and there are none listed for Zambia. I think my best chance of getting something specially made from a design that I would provide would be in South Africa or Kenya.

"Since I have a contact, Frank Minot in the African Wildlife Leadership Foundation in Nairobi, I will try to call him to see what he can find out about plastic manufacturers in Kenya. He told me to call him if I needed help in obtaining items for the Luangwa Survey, so I will try him first."

I went into the reception room, gave Frank's office number to Yvonne, and asked her to make the call to Nairobi. As usual, all telephone lines were busy, but the operator said that there was no one waiting right now so the Game Department was first for a vacant line. I went back into my room to open some mail that had been placed on my desk. In the stack was a handwritten letter from I.S. Jasat asking if Joshua Njovo was an employee of mine. He wanted to confirm the employment because Joshua wanted to buy a bicycle on credit. Jasat further wanted to know if I would co-sign an agreement with him to pay for the bicycle if Joshua defaulted. I had just finished the note when Yvonne came in to let me know that Frank Minot was on the line. I went into her office and put the receiver to my ear.

"Hello Frank, I bet you did not expect to hear from me so soon, but I need some help in finding a plastics company in Nairobi that might be able to make an ear tag for an elephant."

There was a long pause, and for a minute I thought the connection had been broken.

"Well, I have heard about many crazy projects in Africa, but this may be the most unusual one."

I spent the next ten minutes explaining what I wanted to do and how an elephant's ear has an excellent spot for the right type of ear tag.

Frank listened to my story and said, "It might just work, and I'll try to find what you need here in Nairobi so give me the details."

"What I need is a round disk that measures ten inches in diameter with a hole in the center that is three-eighths-inch and a large number engraved on the front surface. You may have seen the laminated name tags used by businesses to identify their employees; these tags have two layers. The first layer is the color of the number and the second layer is cut through to the first. In our case the first layer must be white and the second layer red. In this manner it will appear as a red tag with white numbers.

"In addition I need a stainless steel three-eighths-inch bolt that is 1.5 to 2.0 inches in length, two washers, two nuts, and one lock washer. The bolt has to have threads that cover three-quarters of the shaft. If you cannot find stainless steel then brass will do."

"What numbers do you want on the tags?" Frank asked.

"I would like numbers 30 to 35 along with sufficient bolts and nuts for these six disks, and this should be enough for this experiment. Below the number I would like the letter Z to indicate Zambia."

Frank said that he would start searching the next day for what I needed and would let me know in several days whether he was successful. He made one last comment as we were nearing the end of our conversation: "If I obtain the items you need and you actually get a tag placed in an elephant's ear then all I want is a photograph of you and the elephant showing the numbered tag in the right spot." With this we said goodbye, and as I hung up the phone I heard him chuckle.

A short time later Joshua came into the office and asked if Jasat Store had contacted me to vouch for his employment. I told him that I just received the note today and had not responded to his request because I was trying to decide what to do as he was not yet on the payroll. For this reason I could not in all honesty tell Jasat that he was employed. Joshua seemed irritated that I would not confirm his employment. I told him that I might send the letter after his job started when we moved into our new office at the edge of town.

"But Jasat has agreed to let me buy a bicycle on credit if you would vouch for me as an employee. I need this bicycle for transportation to get to work from my village."

"Look Joshua, we have discussed this enough for now. I will not talk to you about this any more until we have you on the payroll, so until then you will have to walk as you have done for many years." With that he walked out the door and was not a happy person.

The next day Stan came into the office and said that the new office building to house the Luangwa team would be ready within a week and that we should think about hiring a secretary. He had been informed by radio that the Game Department had ordered office furniture several months back and that it was now ready and would be on the next lorry from Chilanga to Fort Jameson.

"There is a woman whose husband works for the Agriculture Department here in Fort Jameson who is looking for a job. Her name is Patricia Donald, and she would be a good person to hire. If you want, I will make contact with her and ask the question."

I told him to go ahead and ask, and if she was interested she should come to talk to me. Pat came to see me the next day. I explained that the position was mainly a secretary's job consisting of typing our reports, setting up a filing system for the UNDP team that would be there after we leave, paying our bills and running errands, and being our contact with the local government offices. She had a good knowledge of who to contact for what and could point us in the right direction when we had an administrative problem. I offered and she accepted the job to start when we moved to a new office.

A few days later Frank Minot called to let me know that the type of laminated disk that I wanted could be made in Nairobi and it could be in a red that glowed in the dark. I told him to go ahead and place the order and to ship the disks air freight to Fort Jameson by Zambian Airways. It only took a week after placing the order that the ear tags had arrived in Fort Jameson. I received a hand-delivered note from the ticket clerk, Paul Luposa, that he had a package addressed to me. I had become fairly well acquainted with Paul through flying back and forth to Lusaka numerous times and working with him to deliver special mail to the Game Department in Chilanga.

When I opened the package I was pleasantly surprised to find the disks were made exactly as I had wanted. The numbers were very distinct. The hole in the center and the outside edge was very smooth, so the disk should not cause any irritation to the animal. Now I was ready for the experiment. After coordinating the use of a vehicle and getting the schedule set for the marking crew, the day finally arrived when we would try to put an identification tag in an elephant's ear. I met Ian and his two assistants at Mfuwe and unloaded my equipment into their Land Rover. Sam was driving and James would be our gun bearer. We had no idea of how successful we would be the first day out, so I brought adequate supplies just in case we had to stay overnight. Our plan was to drive along the Luangwa River to the Mupamadzi and then head west along a bush track to the edge of the Chifungwe Plain in the Munyamadzi Corridor. This was the area where the Game Department lacked information on elephant movements.

The general area around the Luangwa and Mupamadzi confluence has historical significance because it is along the route of three explorer expeditions: Dr. Livingston's in 1868, J. Da Silva in 1853, and P.J. Baptistsa and A. Jose in 1806. Livingston never made it back from his expedition. He died May 1, 1873, at Chitambo, and his heart was buried there while his servants carried his body to the coast to be returned to England. There was also a major Portuguese trade route from 1550 to 1760 to the interior that came up the Zambezi then overland to meet the Luangwa at Macambo.

Many of the travelers had muzzleloading guns because the route was also one used by slave traders. As a result, over a long time many of these guns found their way into the local African population and are still in use by poachers. One gun I saw that had been confiscated from a poacher was a muzzleloader with dry skin holding the barrel on the stock. The skin came from the leg of an antelope and was stretched over the barrel and stock. When it dried the skin was very tight and held the barrel firmly in place. The butt end had a cross made from thumbtacks driven into the wood, indicating that the owner belonged to the Christian religion.

As we traveled west along the river I could not help but wonder what animals the three explorers saw, what the vegetation was like, and how many people lived there in the mid 1800s. I also wondered what these explorers would say if they had met us along the way in a motorized vehicle, with equipment that they had never seen or even dreamed about, with the objective of putting a tag in an elephant's ear. In a way they were pioneers in their time, trying to discover new things to extend man's knowledge about our world. We were pioneers on a smaller scale, trying to extend our knowledge about animals and how to better manage them so that they will exist in the future.

As a result of the high number of elephants in the north end of the South Reserve and the corridor, it also was an area where elephants raided local gardens and crop damage was high in the villages scattered along the Munyamadzi River. The Game Department was considering moving people from the corridor to reduce the impact on wildlife when the area became part of a national park. The Eastern Province Minister Mbewe was in favor of moving all villages, but he had decided not to make a decision until our survey team submitted a report of our findings and recommendations to the United Nations Development Program and the Government of Zambia.

Our trip north from Mfuwe was slow and deliberate as we observed many single bull elephants and family groups along the way and saw several large buffalo herds. The November rains were still a few weeks away, and traveling off the main dirt road was not a problem. The amazing thing was seeing elephant, buffalo, zebra, giraffe, impala, warthog, waterbuck, baboons, and other smaller species in the general area at the same time and not paying much attention to each other. We did not see any of the big cats, but with the number and population of species present, we were certain that they were not far away.

Tsetse flies were numerous, and their bite feels like a bee sting. We kept several cans of insect spray in the vehicle along with some fly swatters. The spray was used before getting back into the Land Rover when we had stopped to look around, especially if we had been in brushy areas. Our concern about tsetse was well founded as one British VSO who worked at the Kakumba cropping station contacted sleeping sickness. He had been feeling ill for several days and was taken to the Fort Jameson Hospital. The doctors there diagnosed trypanosomiasis and he was given the prescribed medication, which was an arsenic compound, but after several days with a high fever he died. Speculation was going through the expatriate community, spread by one of the attending nurses, that the Indian doctor on duty gave him a higher dose of the medication than usual and that he died as a result of the treatment. After hearing this I decided not to allow an Indian doctor to examine or treat any of my family. From all the information that I could obtain, there was an indication that the Indian doctors in Africa were only marginally qualified.

On the day that the VSO died I was on a flight back from the South Reserve with Robert Lawson. We landed at Fort Jameson, and there was a message for Robert to call CGO. He was given instructions to pick up the body at the African morgue in Fort Jameson and fly it to Lusaka where it would be received by staff from the British Embassy. Stan Stenton came to the airport to transport me to town while Robert stayed with his Cessna to remove the passenger seat. When we got to the morgue Stan was not about to go inside to get the body, so I went in by myself. The morgue was a concrete building with no windows, but it had vents going through the ceiling. Several fans were drawing air from outside that forced the inside air with the oppressive odor out the roof vents. There was one cold storage cabinet that could hold three bodies; it had a small compressor and was located near the front of the building. The rest of the room had concrete slabs about three by six feet and three feet high. There were twenty of these slabs, and more than half had bodies face up with no covers except the clothing they had on at the time of death. All of the bodies had an identification and information tag attached to a big toe. The VSO was wrapped with a white sheet with a red cross on the top and was the only body in the cooler.

One African attendant and I pulled the body out of the cooler onto a gurney held in place by another attendant. As we pulled the body tray out my hands slipped a little along the rail and were wet with body fluid. I immediately wiped them on the white sheet but the smell remained on my hands. We pushed the gurney out the door, and Stan helped me lay the body in the back of a Game Department truck. I had been in the morgue a total of ten minutes and that was about as long as I could stand the odor. I rode in the back of the truck with the body on the way to the airport. Robert met us outside the terminal. The plane had been fueled, and the passenger door was open and ready for the passenger. Robert had already removed the passenger seat, and I helped him place the body in the cabin with the head under the instrument panel on the passenger side. We waited until the plane was airborne and then Stan and I drove back to his office to radio Chilanga that Robert was in the air and on his way to Lusaka with the body.

When I got home and started to get out of the car I noticed that the smell of death had permeated my shirt and pants even though I had been in the morgue just a short time. Before going into the house I removed all my clothing except for my shorts and washed my hands in a bucket of water with disinfectant. I put everything in a burn pit behind my house, soaked them with diesel, and started a fire. As soon as I got in the house I went to the shower room and washed down with lots of soap. Doris brought me clean clothes and I took my shorts to the fire pit. This experience with tsetse and sleeping sickness brought back the reality that I was living in a developing country with a family and there was always an inherent risk of sickness and death.

As our marking crew traveled along the bush track, we went through several burned areas, and in some places there was the slight hint of green plants starting to appear. There had been several light showers in the area, which indicated that the rainy season was not far off. We took our time in moving along the riverine vegetation with an occasional detour through trees and open space just to see what was there. We were still south of the Mupamadzi and in the South Reserve. As we got near Lundu Plain, we started to see young single elephants along with some large mature bulls. Our hope was to find a male that was not a mature adult because these were the ones that traveled over large areas and would provide good movement information.

We eased out of the plain and crossed the river where there was a good rock base and low water. This time of year there were several places to cross, and our Land Rover had large tires with a high clearance so crossing in most places was not a problem. The water was not as muddy in this area because we were only a short distance from the escarpment and the large silt-laden tributaries were not present. We had gone only a short distance outside the Reserve between Lundu and Chifungwe Plain when Sam pointed to a single bull pulling branches from a small group of trees. We had a good view of his posterior, and he had not turned to look at us. Sam put the Rover into low gear for slow movement and eased closer to this bull. When we got within forty yards he still had not made any behavior movements that would indicate he knew that we were there.

My agreement with Stan and Ian was that I would be the shooter on this occasion. I had an ear tag with the number 33, and my age this year was thirty-three. My birthday gift from the Game Department was that I would be given the honor of shooting my first elephant and at the same time putting the first ear tag in an elephant's ear—the one I brought down. This was one birthday present that I would never forget.

James would be my backup, and just in case this did not work, Ian also was carrying a .375 but would remain between James and the vehicle. Stan had suggested the second rifle for protection in case we had threats from other dangerous animals. However, without saying it, he was also concerned about us encountering the human species that may be poaching in the area.

We got out of the Rover and did not shut the doors. James picked up some dusty soil and let it drop from his raised hand. The wind was right and the elephant still had not turned around, so our combined wisdom indicated that it was a go if I could get within twenty yards. Stalking animals was a technique that I had learned years earlier while deer hunting in the mountains of West Virginia—but this was no deer! My movements and actions had to be perfect, and my judgment of the weight of the dart and the amount of drop it would make had to be correct. Ian and James looked around the area for other dangers that might be in the grass or in the bush.

Our field of view was good and they gave me the thumbs up. I started walking slowly toward the young bull, but he sure looked bigger now and a lot more dangerous than at fifty yards. We were within twenty-five yards when his trunk shot up into the air as though he had detected our odor. However, it was not us he detected but a group of villagers walking on a trail off to his left and about seventy-five yards in front. His trunk came down and he continued to pull at some lower branches. I continued the snail's pace until, by my estimation, I was in a good position.

I raised my gun and placed it solidly against my right shoulder. My squeeze was firm and steady, and the gun made the familiar *poof*, at which point the dart hit the rump in the right spot and the barb was holding it in place. He flinched, hunched forward a few feet and, then again extended his trunk upward searching for a scent in the slight breeze that was now starting to come up.

James and I remained quiet, his gun at ready position but mine pointing down. After fifteen minutes, which seemed like an eternity, the bull started to weave. We remained quiet and motionless, but fatigue was starting to have its effects on our muscles from standing so quiet and motionless. He did not move from his spot but went down on his knees and remained still. This was not good because it was possible for him to suffocate because of the pressure on his lungs. As a result, time was critical and we went to work right away to complete our tasks. Total time from shot to put-down was just over fifteen minutes. Ian motioned Sam to bring the vehicle forward and James, Ian, and I walked to the front side of the animal. My thoughts were that if this elephant had a long memory, as the legend goes, then he surely would have imprinted our faces in his mind and would come after us if he ever caught us in the bush again. He was breathing steadily and seemed to be completely out. We were now in business.

"Sam, I need you to start a small fire with the charcoal in this bag. Use some mineral spirits to help get it started," I said. "When the coals are hot, put the copper iron in and get it to a heat that will burn a piece of dry grass. Ian, you go ahead and record the body measurements. James and I will pierce the ear."

I had James hold the block of wood behind the elephant's ear at the center of the curve. I placed the three-eighths-inch steel punch in the curve in the front and hit it several times with the hammer, which caused James to jerk just a little. The wood was not heavy enough to form a solid base for the punch to penetrate easily, but it was also not hard enough to damage the ear. Previously I had used a file to sharpen the punch and tried it on several pieces of thick leather and it accomplished the job. The thing I did not know was how hard it would be to punch through living skin and cartilage. It took several hits with the hammer to get the punch through to the wood, but it worked, and there was only a small trickle of blood.

"James, check the iron to see if it is hot," I said. James took the iron by its wooden handle and touched it to a piece of grass, which immediately caught fire.

"That looks good," I said. "Now give it to me."

I touched the skin around the hole both front and back to cauterize the flesh. I also went around the elephant and eased the dart out of the rump and cauterized the small opening. After this was done I pasted the ear hole with petroleum jelly to lubricate the inside before inserting the bolt. Next, I put a washer on the bolt, inserted the bolt through the ear tag and the hole in the ear, and put on another washer and held it in place with a nut. I hand tightened the nut but left space for movement of the bolt. At this point I placed a lock washer over the bolt and then tightened it with another nut. While holding the first nut in place with a spanner, I tightened the second nut to squeeze down the lock washer for a firm hold.

The elephant now had a permanent ear tag. Although the tag had the number 33 to commemorate my birthday, I thought that identifying this majestic animal just by a number was sort of degrading, so I gave him the name "Chifungwe" to identify him with the area where he was captured. As a precaution, if the tag came off, I painted a large white spot on his back so that we could spot him easily from the air to check on his well-being for the next few weeks if the paint lasted that long.

"Sam, let's get all the equipment back into the vehicle while Ian prepares a dart with M285," I said. "However, before we load up, I need you to take a photograph of me holding Chifungwe's ear with his new tag." I handed Sam my 35mm camera, and he took the pictures of proof that I needed to send to Frank Minot and it was my turn to chuckle.

"Ian, when we get everything in the Rover, give him the shot and jump in so we can get out of his way quickly."

Ian inserted the syringe into a big vein on his right ear and pushed the plunger. He got into the vehicle, and we moved off to about fifty yards. In a few minutes Chifungwe was standing but a little wobbly. He stood there for a few more minutes and then slowly started to walk off toward the Muchinga escarpment. The ear tag was very visible, and he would be easily identified from the air and on the ground if he were facing an observer.

Since our light was getting dimmer we decided to remain for the night. We made a dry camp and opened several tins of corned beef and some tins of peaches purchased from Jasat. In addition we celebrated our success by drinking several warm bottles of Lion beer that I had brought along for the occasion. Warm beer had never been my favorite beverage, but after several times of having it in the bush I was beginning to actually like it that way.

Now that the marking job was accomplished, I had one final thing to do, and that was to identify the capture location on my set of the aerial photographs that were made in 1965. I had brought my stereoscope for this purpose, so I set it up on the top of our equipment box and looked at the stereo pairs. I found the location based on some visible topographic features, and I put a needle through the spot. On the backside of the photograph at the pinhole I wrote the tag number, date, time, conditions, and members of the marking crew along with the measurements Ian had recorded. This photograph would be a permanent record of marking the elephant. After finishing with the photographs we talked for several hours. I did most of the talking by answering questions from Sam and James about what it was like living in the U.S. and how would I compare the different ways of rural living.

By answering their numerous questions, I think that we came to a better understanding of each other and our relationship and that would help us work better as a team. Ian would soon be leaving for the U.S. because he had been accepted into the wildlife program at Colorado State University to work on a bachelor's degree, and I would take over the job of supervising the marking crew.

My idea was that each of us would take turns at night watch, but Sam had a different opinion. "Being on guard is mine and James's job. You and Ian are responsible for the technical work, and we are responsible for your safety, and that is the way it should be. We will each stand watch at two-hour intervals." Sam said.

"Go to bed when you want, and we will talk to you again in the morning," James said. The night sky was clear and we were tired, so it was not difficult to fall asleep on our small safari cots made of steel frames and canvas. Because we were in a malaria area we had mosquito nets, but I was the only one that put mine to use. I was also the only one that took a chloroquine tablet once a week. The noises of the night are something that one never forgets, especially the sounds of lions roaring. Even though they are at a distance, the sound travels and it still made me uneasy even though we had a Game Guard on watch. Before coming to Zambia, I had read a story about the man-eating lions of Tsavo, and from this account I had developed a healthy respect for this animal with the goal that I would not become a victim of any man-eating lions of the South Game Reserve.

Morning came early and we had corned beef for breakfast but no warm beer. James had started a small fire with charcoal to boil water for tea, and this really tasted good. After getting ourselves awake and fed, we loaded the Rover and set out toward the escarpment and then south to the middle of the Reserve to Mfuwe. For several days we would not try to locate Chifungwe from the ground to reduce stress and give him a chance to fully recover from the trauma of being immobilized. The time was necessary to see if the tag remained in the ear. I did not want to tag any more animals at this time; instead I wanted to know that our procedure worked before putting the tags into other elephants' ears.

During the entire route we saw many elephants and one especially large one. The large bull had tusks that almost touched the ground, which made him look something like a spider with six legs. Ian said that this bull actually had the nickname of "Spider" and only a few Game Department people knew of his presence. He certainly was a magnificent specimen, and as luck would have it I had already used all of our film. When my office was in the Game Department warehouse I had access to a large number of tusks that had their weight marked with paint on the ivory. These tusks were all from natural mortality and were found in and around the South Game Reserve from 1961 to 1966. Of 187 tusks only one was over 100 pounds. The tusks we saw on Spider looked like this one.

We arrived back at Mfuwe late in the afternoon, and I decided to go on to Fort Jameson. I removed all of my equipment and personal gear from the Land Rover and transferred it to my vehicle on loan from the Department.

"I want to thank each of you for your efforts yesterday," I said to Ian, Sam, and James. "One of my main jobs now is to keep account of sightings as well as flying the area to locate Chifungwe. I probably will need one of you each time I fly because Robert Lawson may not be available, but I can rent his plane."

That statement came as a surprise because I had not told anyone that I had a license to fly a single-engine plane. Before I left, Sam pulled me off to the side and told me that he was certain that we had been watched during the tagging process. Although he never saw anyone, his bush instincts told him someone was out there watching Chifungwe during the same time that we were there. I told him not to be concerned and that it was probably because he was just tired from being on guard duty and I let it go at that.

Chapter Nine

We were notified by the Public Works Department that we could move into the new office space. Water and electricity had already been connected and a septic system installed for sewage. It would take a long time to get approval for a telephone, so we would still have to go to the Game Department Office to make calls. Our new office building, on a piece of land designated for Game Department use, was along the road to the provincial minister's house, and the road was always in good repair.

I let Joshua and Pat know that we were now ready to move into our new building. It took about half a day to get everything moved from the warehouse, my house, and my temporary office to the new building. The room that I would occupy had plenty of space for a desk and several large tables where I could sort out and group all the old documents that I was studying as background material for our report. One table was completely devoted to aerial photo and map interpretation.

On one wall I had a bulletin board with a map of the survey area that I used to mark locations of all immobilized elephants, including Chifungwe. This map was a copy of the official location map that had been started by the marking crew and kept in the radio room at the Game Department's Office. Each marked animal had a reference file with information that pertained to the animal's capture site, all sightings and locations, and biological information.

Joshua came to the office riding a bicycle. "Where did you get the new bicycle?" I asked.

"Jasat agreed that since I was now working that he would go ahead and give me the bicycle on account," he said.

"Well, your account was arranged with Jasat without my signature and is really none of my business, but I encourage you to be on time with your payments.

"However, since you will be using your own bicycle for running errands for us I will give you a monthly allowance for its use." With that said I gave him several official letters to take to the Game Department for mailing.

My first job of the day was to go to the Game Department to let Stan know that we had an elephant with an ear tag. I drove to the office and took Pat with me so that she could call Robert Lawson. We arrived at the office just as Stan was getting ready to review his Game Guards before they went out on patrol.

Before I could say anything Stan said, "I hear that you were successful in getting a tag in an elephant's ear. Congratulations, to be frank, I never thought you could do it."

"Thanks for the confidence," I said. "How did you find out about the successful tagging?" I asked.

"We had several Game Guards come up from Mfuwe, and they were talking about this elephant with a red thing in its ear.

"Ian's assistants had told them about you putting the elephant down and placing this round plastic disk in its ear," Stan said.

"Now that the word is out among the Game Department employees I need to talk to Norman Carr so that he will not let any of his hunting clients kill the animal.

"He is not of trophy size anyway, but he is now unique among elephants," I said. "Am I correct in assuming that Norman has the hunting rights for the corridor?" I asked Stan.

"That is right. He was given the concession for 66 and 67 for hunting and walking safaris."

"One more thing before I go. During your review today, would you inform the Guards, while they are doing their tour in the corridor, to be on the watch for number 33 and write down his location by referencing it to a landmark that we can locate on our map? Also, if you call Chilanga today, let CGO know of Chifungwe. That is what I call him because of where he was captured, but I do not know what it means in Nyanja."

"Okay I'll let the Guards know, and they will collect the location information that you need," Stan said. "And you better let Norman know today because he has already informed me that they have two hunting clients going out this week."

Pat had tried to call Robert Lawson, but the lines were all in use for the next thirty minutes. I told her to stay around until she could get a call through and that if I were not back by then to ask Robert to meet me at the Fort Jameson airport on Wednesday to fly the Valley. If he could not make the trip then he was to give me the next date that he could fly.

From the Game Department I went directly to Luangwa Safaris. Mrs. Leach-Lewis greeted me at the desk, and I asked if Norman was in town.

"He is and I will let him know you are here," she said.

"David, it is good to see you again. What can I do for you?" Norman asked.

"Mainly I just wanted to alert you that I have an elephant marked with an ear tag with the number 33. You will be receiving an official letter from the Game Department putting this particular animal off limits to hunters, but it would be okay to get a look at the tag with tourists on a walking safari if you run into him. The tag is clearly visible, and we would not want to lose this animal to an anxious hunter," I said. "He is not a trophy animal, and I doubt that any serious hunter would consider him anyway."

"I appreciate the information. We do have two hunters to take out at the end of this week that have elephant licenses," Norman said.

"Also I would appreciate it, if you do see him, that you note the location and tie it to a landmark that I can identify on our large map in my office. Over the next few months we hope to plot the locations of this elephant and see where he moves in and out of the Game Reserves," I said.

"I would like to go out with you sometime when you plan on marking another elephant. I had to kill a lot of animals when I was on control work in my early years with the Department. But this would be a lot of fun, to actually shoot an animal and then bring him back to life again," Norman said.

"We will plan on a trip in a couple of weeks, and I will let you know ahead of time so you can go with me if the time is okay for you," I told him.

When I returned to the office, Pat said that she was able to talk to Robert Lawson and that he would meet me at the airport at 8:00 A.M. on Wednesday. Joshua had returned from the Game Department, and I asked him to meet with me and Pat for a few minutes. Since Pat would be there when I was out in the reserves, I wanted someone to monitor Joshua's work and to assign tasks to keep him occupied. Joshua and Pat came into my room, and I noticed him looking at the location chart that I had started on elephant number 33.

"What does all this mean?" he asked. "And why are you capturing elephants?"

It took a while to explain, but while Pat was there I wanted her to hear what I told Joshua about the Luangwa Survey and what our team would be doing for the next year. During her interview we did not get into the details of the survey, but since she would be doing most of the typing of our reports, I thought that she should know what the outcome would be and how important her job was to our success. Joshua wanted to keep asking questions about my work, especially how to tag and keep track of elephants, but my main purpose of this meeting was to let him know that, when I was not there, Pat would assign his duties. He did not seem to like this idea but did not voice a strong objection. To get him started I told him to start cleaning the other office that would be occupied by the team member who would be arriving in a couple of weeks.

I met Robert Lawson at the airport at 8:00 A.M. as planned. Up till now Robert had done all the flying because I was not too familiar with the landscape or landmarks except for the flight over the reserves with Rhodes and Uys. Today I would be the pilot and Robert the observer. My skills at flying were a little rusty because I had not been in the pilot's seat since leaving Arizona. We topped off the tanks, and I taxied to the run-up point to check that generators and instruments were working properly and to listen to what the engine was saying to us. I moved the controls right, left, up, down, and set the flaps.

The weather was cool and there was no wind, so the day looked good for flying and observing. I checked that I had my binoculars and Bronica camera and aerial photographs for the area we were going to cover. No planes had contacted the tower and we could not see any in sight, so I lined up on the dirt runway and pushed the throttle forward. The plane responded and we were on our way. The airfoil was lifting, and the plane wanted to go up; I gently pulled back on the control, and we were immediately in the air.

I set a course to cross over the Luangwa River and northwest to get to the border of the South Reserve. We were at 5,000 feet but descended to 3,500 over the Lundu Plain toward the escarpment to start our search for Chifungwe. I dropped down another 500 feet when I saw several scattered elephants and started a slow turn to get them to respond by looking up. Almost all of them were the right size, but no red showed in any left ear. I nosed the plane up to gain altitude to get a better field of view and remained on a southeast course for another ten to fifteen minutes. There were several herds of twenty to thirty animals along with family groups, but no Chifungwe. Buffalo herds were scattered around the landscape, and we saw giraffe feeding in the tops of acacia trees. I headed northeast to catch the middle of the Munyamadzi. We were still seeing the right size of elephant but not the one that we wanted. When we got to the Mupamadzi in the middle of the corridor I made a slight left turn to look over the Chifungwe Plain area to get some photographs. There were several nice herds of both elephant and buffalo in front of us, and the light was very good.

"Robert, get the Bronica out, and set the shutter speed at five hundredths of a second. Set the light meter to that speed and see what f stop reading you get."

"The meter reads 5.6," he said.

"I'll move over to the left of the herd that will be coming up in a few minutes. Be ready to snap as we go by."

I lowered the flaps a little to slow down, Robert took two shots, and we continued past the herd. At that point I headed for the road track that came down the escarpment and continued to Nabwalya. We saw several people walking the road, but there were no vehicles. However, the road looked like it had been used more lately, and this probably would continue until the rains started in the fall.

"You know, David, the Chinese are helping Zambia build the railway to Tanzania with a connection all the way to Kenya.

"There is speculation among some of the locals in Mpika that Tanzanian, and maybe Chinese, workers are visiting the corridor and have started to buy small quantities of ivory from the villagers," Robert said.

Nodding to indicate my understanding I said, "I'll check discreetly within the Game Department to see what others know about this. Thanks for letting me know."

I made a slow turn to the left to go back into the South Reserve and several miles south of the course that we followed from Fort Jameson. The weather was still very good with clear sky, but far off to the east you could see the seeds of small cumulus clouds starting to appear. It would not be long before the rains would start. Our course would eventually take us over the Luambe Reserve on the east bank and on to Fort Jameson. We were about halfway along the river course that drained into the Luangwa just opposite the west boundary of Luambe. Robert touched me on the shoulder and pointed. There were several scattered single elephants off to the right of the plane.

"The animals appear to be about the right size, so maybe we should check them out," he said. I nosed the plane down and added some flap. We were about 300 feet overhead, and they were starting to turn around to face the noise. There were about eight animals that we could see with several more straight ahead. None of the eight had the thing in their ear, but I caught a flash of red when we passed over the remaining two, and one quickly turned, shook his head, and then returned to his previous direction. I wondered if my eyes were playing tricks or if I just wanted to see Chifungwe so badly that imagination was a factor. The only way to be sure was to get some space between us by going ahead and doing a 180 to check him out face on. I made the turn, and Robert could hardly contain himself.

"It's him," he said in a very enthusiastic voice. The ear tag was clearly visible, but the white spot on his back could only be detected up close and was now almost gone. Sure enough we had located Chifungwe headed east in the direction of Luambe. I had the aerial photographs in my lap and drew an approximate location in pencil on the photograph. I would make a pinhole later to show the location and give it a number, as well as describing the topographic features, weather, etc., on the reference card for this sighting. With Robert using the binoculars we made several passes over Chifungwe to check for any sign of injury. He looked in good physical condition, and we had accomplished our goal for the day. With a great sense of accomplishment we crossed the Luangwa at about 200 feet, right over a large pool with lots of hippo. I made a mental note that this is one pool that I had to see on the ground.

About twenty minutes out I contacted the Fort Jameson tower and asked for a refueling truck to meet us at the terminal. We arrived back at Fort Jameson—and just in time, as the fuel gauge was nearing empty. The windsock was hanging down. I lined up with the runway and pulled back on the throttle, set the trim, and let the plane settle down to a smooth landing. The fuel truck was there, and the driver started filling the tank. I told Robert that we needed to have a regular schedule for the next few months and that I would figure this out and give him a call. The truck driver brought me the bill, and I signed for the fuel under a Game Department account. Robert remarked that it had been a very exciting day, and I watched as he got in his plane and took off for Mpika.

Chapter Ten

Sam came to my office alone one afternoon and wanted to talk. He had walked from the Game Department, which was a couple of miles away, so I knew his coming to see me had to be important. We chatted several minutes about how he liked what he was doing and the fact that he was helping to collect information that would eventually result in recommendations to the government that could help people in rural areas. I could tell that there was something else bothering him and he just needed to get to the point where he felt comfortable in discussing the subject.

"You know the day we put the ear tag in the elephant's ear and I told you that I had a feeling someone was watching?"

"Yes, I remember; is there still something troubling you about that day?"

"It is not so much of me or you being watched, but I have this strong feeling that someone else is always following our elephant and knows his location as well or better than we do. I have family and friends in the corridor that I trust, and they tell me that they hear stories about the elephant with a red ear that has powerful medicine.

"This elephant is important to me and to the FAO project and I am concerned that because of his reputation some people will try to do him harm. They believe that animals have magic power and that this power is transferred to you when you kill an animal and perform the appropriate ritual. Many hunters believe they have magic that makes them invisible to the animal they are hunting and they practice this magic. These rituals are only known to medicine men and certain hunters," he explained.

"Sam, I appreciate your concern, but I do not know what we can do other than one of us follow the elephant all the time, and this would be difficult."

"There is another way, and that is why I am here," he said. "My family's friends in the corridor would be willing to listen and pass on information to you and watch the animal for us for a few days at a time if we can first locate him from the air. They know the corridor and northern part of the Luangwa South Reserve very well.

"In their youth their dad was a Bisa hunter, and he taught them how to behave like the animal they want to track, and they practiced for many years stalking animals, including elephants, in the Game Reserves.

"They are very trustworthy and want to become Game Guards for the Department, and this would be one way for them to show their interest and trust."

"Sam, I believe everything that you have told me, but this may be beyond our capabilities to bring about. However, because of your concern, why don't we meet these friends of yours and talk about how they would keep track of our "gray ghost," as some villagers call him.

"Because there are obviously many people that have an interest in Chifungwe besides us, we need to keep our activities known to only a few people to include you, me, James, and Stan. How do we make contact with your friends without anyone else knowing?"

"I will contact them in my own way," Sam said. "When and where would you like to meet them?"

"I think the best thing is for our crew to make a trip to the Valley and pick up your friends walking on the road inside the Luambe Reserve. We will not cross the river so that we will be out of the South Reserve to lessen the chances of someone seeing them with us. Let's try to meet next week on Friday, and that will give me time to think of some possibilities and options. We will meet them on the road at about 10:00 A.M. In the meantime, do not say anything to anyone."

I asked Sam if I could take him back to the Game Department, and he indicated that this would save him some time because he had to get the contact process in place starting today. He got in my vehicle, and I drove him to the Department's warehouse and let him out. This was not an unusual occurrence, so no one would think anything was different. On our way Sam was quiet and I could tell he was deep in thought, and I was also thinking to myself that I hoped I was doing the right thing. Sam was a dedicated employee, and I should not question his motives or his desire to help.

My thinking was that something had to happen to show that Chifungwe was protected from people who wanted to do him harm because he could sense their intention. Something that Sam said was beginning to form the basis of a plan that was simple, sort of a wild idea but, like the ear tag, might just work.

During the week I talked to Stan about the problem of Chifungwe becoming a notorious animal and that Sam was certain that hunters in the corridor were starting to think that they could bring him down and get his power. Stan said that several local government officials had received complaints about the elephant with the red ear raiding their gardens, and some hunters had even complained that he was taking away their magic to hunt. I told Stan what I was going to do, and he expressed reservations about being successful but that anything that would keep Chifungwe alive was worth a try.

We left Fort Jameson early and arrived in the Luambe Reserve on time. Just as Sam promised, there were two young men walking on the road. Sam recognized his friends right away as David Tembo and Christian Chalikulima. David and Tembo are both common names in East Africa, while Christian is less common, and Chalikulima is not well known. Sam had already told me that both lived in a village east of Nabwalya but only several miles from the Luangwa River. They had attended the government school in Nabwalya and could speak English well and write in a broken structure. David was about twenty-two and Christian was about twenty-five, but Sam said that he did not know their exact age.

We drove into Luambe Reserve and stopped at a table near one of the round brick tourist huts. These huts date back to the fifties and were originally built by Norman Carr. I asked both David and Christian why they wanted to help us protect the marked elephant. Christian talked for both of them and said that they wanted to be Game Guards for the Department and had helped the Guards who were stationed in Nabwala several times when they were on animal control work. In particular they had tracked elephants that were constantly raiding gardens near their village. Sam had already explained what we were doing in the Luangwa Valley, and they responded that they wanted to be part of something that would help them get experience that might be beneficial in getting a job.

"It is easy to follow elephants once you decide which one you want to track," Christian said. "We can follow an animal for several weeks at a time and never lose him."

"The concern I have is that you can follow the animal and stay near him, but what happens when he is confronted by people who want to kill him for his magic?" I said. "This is extremely dangerous and either of you could be killed, and we have no weapons for you to carry for protection."

"We will have our spears and bows, " David said.

"Spears and bows do not match the weapons that some of the poachers have, and I cannot take the chance of you being killed. However, there is another way that I want you to think about that is safe and could solve the problem. Sam has told me that you were trained by your dad in the traditional ways of hunting but that you do not believe in magic or medicine as do other hunters; why is this?" I asked.

"We learned in school that there is no such thing as medicine and magic, and both of us are Christians and do not accept the old ways of hunting," David said.

"I asked this question because I did not want to cause you any problem in what I am proposing, and you do not have to accept the idea. Knowing that most of the hunters are superstitious, I propose that we start a rumor through the corridor that our elephant can detect when someone wants to do him harm, he can take away all the medicine and magic they possess, and they will not be able to make themselves invisible when hunting. My question to the two of you is: Thinking of yourselves as being a hunter who believes in magic, would you try to kill the animal with the red ear if you heard that rumor in the corridor?"

Both David and Christian responded at the same time with a "No, the belief in magic is too strong to take a chance of losing it by getting too close to the elephant."

"The question that I must now ask is: Will this work?"

David indicated that he thought so, depending on whether they could make the rumor credible. Christian said that they would have to select the right people—those who like to talk and gossip without questioning the truth of the information.

With the answers that they provided, I decided to give it a try. "You know who these people are, so the rest is up to you. My suggestion is to start very slowly and spread the rumor a little at a time as you travel through the corridor in the areas where you are commonly known."

I explained to David and Christian that I would pay them eight pounds a month to keep the rumor going and would give them letters of reference to the Game Department for employment. We got back into the Toyota and drove to where we had picked them up. I said, "Please keep in touch by contacting Sam, and don't make any effort to contact me." They agreed, and Sam and I left for Fort Jameson.

While driving back I was reflecting to myself what we had learned from our marked elephant so far. By coordinating aerial locations with ground crews we were able to observe Chifungwe's activities several times. I was interested in his daily routine because I wanted as much life history information as I could collect in hopes that some part of what I observed would be significant for management purposes. Chifungwe spent a lot of time doing what elephants like to do, and that is eating. He ranged widely in the rainy season, eating mostly low vegetation of grasses with an occasional reaching up into the trees for leaves and woody material.

During the dry season his diet was reversed, with the majority of forage coming from trees but frequently picking up something small from the ground. It was amazing how he could put the tip of his trunk on the ground and pick up something to eat that could not be seen even with binoculars.

These morsels certainly must have tasted good but could not have added much to his dietary needs. An elephant of his size would need to consume about three hundred pounds of vegetation a day to maintain his body weight.

Favorite habitats were edges created by trees, brush, and converging grassland, especially along the rivers where water was also available. Chifungwe was not unusual in any way except for the ear tag. He often mingled with other bulls his age and older but also was observed several times as a loner. For the period that we kept track of him, he was not in the musth reproduction condition, so observations of his sexual activities were lacking.

Physically he was not handicapped, and in two instances we saw him take off after people who got too close. We assumed these people were trying to get close enough to see the red ear a little better. Elephants of his stature can easily overtake a human running and can close the distance very quickly. He may have become more sensitive to humans after being immobilized, but this was a factor we could not determine with a sample of one elephant. Although Chifungwe took many trips through the game reserves and up and down the Munyamadzi Corridor, it was obvious that the Chifungwe Plain area was his favorite stomping ground. My information from aerial census also indicated that the plain and connecting forest land north and south was an important habitat for many elephants and was an area that must be included in a new national park when it was established.

We arrived back at the office, and I saw Joshua cleaning around the windows and tables; he was looking at the map showing the locations of number 33. For some reason he had on a nice shirt with a tie, and I asked what was the occasion for the neat appearance.

He responded, "After work I am going to visit my girlfriend, and then I am going to Mpika to attend a local UNIP meeting, but I will be back by Monday morning."

It was at this point that he made a request to have a three-day weekend once a month so that he could travel with the local UNIP leaders in the Eastern Province. I told him it would be okay but that he would have to make up the hours by working when I needed him to be there after five or sometimes on Saturday. I thought this was a reasonable request, and I did not want to give the appearance that our team was not supportive of his participation in the political system.

Near closing time Pat came in with a letter for me from the shipping company that our two Toyotas had been delivered to Beira, Mozambique. I asked her to send a telegram to the company to confirm that the vehicles had arrived and asked that they ship them to Salima, Malawi, by rail. It would take several days for the vehicles to arrive in Malawi, and in the meantime I would have to make arrangements for insurance.

For several weeks I had been promising my family to take them on a trip to the South Reserve to see the different species of wildlife, and it was time to keep this promise. We got up early and drove to Mfuwe. The morning was misty and cool, which kept the dust settled on the road. Our winter rains would soon increase in intensity, and the roads would get worse but not impassable. Most of the fires along the road had quieted down or were snuffed out by the moisture, and the haze from smoke had cleared out. Low vegetation along the route had started to get a green tint, and this meant that soon the animals would start dispersing over the countryside.

When we arrived at the pontoon, the power team was there waiting for business, but one member was missing. I asked where their friend was, and the older of the two young men said that a crocodile had killed his sister while she was washing clothes in the river just north of the Nsefu Reserve. He would be away for several weeks to be with his family for a period of grieving.

It is generally a custom following the death of a family member that relatives help with the expenses of taking care of the deceased person. It is also the custom for the employer of the dead person to give money to the family, and this is also generally expected of friends.

Since I had been across the river and talked to the pontoon crew on many occasions, it probably was expected that I contribute to the funeral fund and I thought that I would do this on the way back.

The hippos were very noisy that morning, and Myra made her usual sound talking back. Over a period of time she actually got very good at imitating their vocalizations. We arrived at the bank and drove off to the road going to Lion Camp. This was an area where most species could be seen without exception, but this did not include leopard or cheetah. This drive was a favorite route for tourists, and that day we were tourists. By then I had learned a lot about the African bush, and the three girls were always asking questions about what they saw. If I did not know the answer, I made it a point to find out because it was also a learning process for me.

Along the road we saw the usual species of impala, zebra, and puku but were treated to the sight of a female giraffe browsing on an acacia tree while her young calf was trying to nurse. We watched for a few minutes then moved away because I had made a practice of not staying for more than a few minutes to watch some species of animals that had young.

As we moved along the road we saw trees that had fruit about a foot long and four inches wide that hung down from the branches. These fruits look just like a large sausage and the tree is appropriately named, sausage tree. Off to our right were several large termite mounds with the cone shape and red color from the underlying soil containing a lot of clay. At the beginning of the rainy season, termites leave their nests to reproduce and are considered a delicacy by the local people. Termites also have an ecological function by relocating soil and adding organic material to its content. It is not uncommon to see a tree or several large bushes growing out of a termite mound.

There were several places along the road to Lion Camp where trees and other vegetation were right up to the edge and might obstruct the view of the area. I was in one of these situations as I was going around a curve and did not see a female elephant with a calf that had just crossed the road off to my left about twenty yards away. The first thing she did was turn and, with a loud trumpet, came at the vehicle. Fortunately the road was straight after the turn, and I pushed the gear into second and put my foot to the pedal and got out of her way. This shook up Doris, but the girls thought it was great. So far our day in the reserve had been exciting, but I did not need any more contact with elephants like that one and I was determined to keep to areas where I had a good view of the surrounding vegetation.

As we moved along the road I went off on a track that went through open areas along the Luangwa River so we could get out of the vehicle and safely walk around. We stopped just opposite a large pool, but we were on an elevated bank and had a good view of the river. I had seen this pool from the air and knew that it would have a large number of hippos, and that is what I had wanted the girls to see. The water was a chocolate color, created by the upwelling of the river bottom as a result of the interactions of this large number of animals. Even though the rains were starting there had not been enough precipitation to increase the water level. Many of the hippos had large scars and cuts on their backs, and some were deep enough to show the underlying white from fat just under the skin.

It was nearing the time that we needed to start back to Mfuwe and I wanted to go back a different way, so I drove off the main road to a track that was away from the river but not in dense vegetation.

On this route we passed a dambo that had dried up but still contained the remains of a young elephant that had become stuck in the mud. The body was covered with white droppings from vultures, but there were still a few picking at the skin and bones. I stopped the vehicle and walked over to the remains to see if there was any ivory in the skull. If it had ivory once it was no longer there, and I returned to the vehicle and started back down the road. Along the way we saw lots of warthogs, and many were females with young. Warthogs were always fun to watch because of the way they ran with their tail sticking straight up like a small flagpole.

I followed this track away from the river until it connected back to the main road to Mfuwe. Because the girls had been awake since five in the morning, I decided we would eat our sandwiches in the vehicle on the way back to Fort Jameson and get there before dark and for an early supper. We arrived back at the pontoon, but it was at the other side. Once the power team saw my Game Department vehicle, they started applying their skill pulling against the cable to get across and our vehicle loaded on board. When we reached the other bank, I took an envelope out of my briefcase and wrote a note saying the enclosed money was for Mboya's family and gave it to the oldest man with instructions that it was to go to their other crew member. He understood, and I was certain that the envelope would be delivered because both of the power team knew that I would be back again when their friend had returned to work. I gave the two workers several books of matches and drove off the pontoon and headed for Fort Jameson.

Chapter Eleven

Salima is a four-hour drive from Fort Jameson and is an easy trip over a dirt and sometimes dusty road, but this first part of the trip would be made by plane. I had Pat call Robert Lawson to determine if he could fly us there, and we scheduled the trip for the next morning. Since there were two vehicles to be picked up, I had to have another driver and Ian was available. Robert met us at 6:30 A.M. at the airport, and we flew to Salima. I did not want to be the pilot that day because we would be crossing the boundary of another country and landing at their airport. Robert had been to Malawi several times and knew the drill associated with international flights in private planes. The airport was seven miles from town, and Robert left us there on our own because he had to get back to Zambia.

When we arrived at the airport we had some unbelievable luck as Ian saw a man he knew on a casual basis, and he gave us a lift to town to the rail station where we saw the Toyotas. Everything appeared to be all right except that there was no petrol in the tanks, the seats were not together, and they did not have tops.

The stationmaster was an Indian named Tovey Sim. He gave me the keys and told me I would have to clear the vehicles with the customs agent across the street. I went to the agent's office and completed all the necessary forms. I asked the agent about a license to drive the Toyotas in Malawi and across the border to Zambia. He said that I did not need a license as long as I had the customs clearance papers.

I was about to leave his office when Tovey called the agent and told him not to let me have the papers until I paid the shipping charges from Beira to

Salima. This was really unexpected because FAO had prepaid all shipping charges for the vehicles to reach Fort Jameson. I did not bring much money with me and I was at a loss to what to do. The customs agent told me that the clearing office was part of the F.C. Smith Co. The previous week I had talked to a representative of the F.C. Smith Co. in Fort Jameson about insurance to drive the Toyotas to Zambia. FAO had taken out insurance with Lloyds of London, but it was good only in Zambia. Mr. Norris of the F.C. Smith Co. was going to write the insurance for me. I called Mr. Norris and explained my situation and asked him if he could pay the shipping charges and told him that he could bill FAO. The customs agent got Norris's authorization over the telephone to pay Tovey the charges.

We had to get some local help to push the vehicles to a petrol station and filled both Toyotas' tanks. One started right off, but the other had a bad battery, which I had to replace. I did not anticipate having to spend so much money on a battery in addition to the petrol, and I ran out of cash. However, the station owner gave me the petrol on credit. He had never seen me in his life but advanced the credit solely on my being an American and he trusted me to send him a check. This certainly was a new experience for me, because everyone in Zambia wanted cash no matter what nationality you were. We were finally able to get both Toyotas running well enough to head for Zambia.

Everything went well until we decided to stop in Lilongwe, Malawi, to get something to eat. Lilongwe only had one hotel, so we parked the Toyotas outside on the street and went in to get some sandwiches. We were busy filling our stomachs when two policemen walked in and asked if we were driving the Toyotas. I said yes and that we were taking them to Zambia for the United Nations. The major asked if I had license plates and registration. I showed him the customs clearance papers and told him that I was told a license was not necessary. He said that I was driving illegally and could not proceed to Zambia until I had a license on both Toyotas. He also said I needed insurance and wanted to see the papers. I explained that Lloyds of London insured me and FAO had the papers. This was not good enough, and the officer said I had better get insurance with the license and since the office was closed I would have to wait until tomorrow.

As luck would have it the F.C. Smith Co. also had an office in Lilongwe, and the agent there agreed to come to the hotel and write the insurance. After he gave me the papers, the police got into their Land Rover and said they would be back in about thirty minutes. I called the warden in Fort Jameson and told him we were on our way but he might send someone to meet us at the border because I was not sure we could get the Toyotas into Zambia without a license.

As soon as I made the call, Ian and I took off for the border, which was an hour away. On the way it started to rain, and I was getting very wet and a little cold since the air had cooled. All the time we were driving I kept looking back afraid the police would be after us when they found out that we had left the hotel. We arrived at the border, and I went to clear Malawi customs. I knew if I got past this stop we would have it made.

The border agent looked at my papers and started filling out his record when he asked me for the license numbers. I explained that the vehicles had a GRZ (Government of the Republic of Zambia) number but that they would be assigned in Fort Jameson. He looked a little puzzled, but when he saw that the Toyotas were new he passed them through. He checked my passport and stamped it EXIT after I explained that I had flown into Malawi from Zambia in a private plane.

There were three border crossings from Fort Jameson to Malawi which we had to go through; two were in Malawi. The first stop was an informal check of vehicles. The boy on the gate knew me from previous trips, so I had no trouble going through. I was very relieved to arrive at the Zambian border and get my passport stamped for reentry. It had now been ten hours since leaving Fort Jameson, and I was getting tired. On my way I met Stan Stenton. He had been kind enough to come after me in his own car, but everything finally had worked out all right.

I arrived home at about 6:00 P.M. and Doris made me some hot tea. While I was relaxing, Tembo came through the back door. He asked if I could go to Fort Jameson Hospital to pick up his mother and drive her to his village. His mother had been taken to the hospital with a broken arm, and she had been released but he had no way to get her home. I told him that I would take her to his village, and we went to the free hospital to pick her up. Both of us had to help her into the Toyota. She was an elderly woman and seemed very feeble. It took about an hour to get to the village.

When we arrived I got out of the Toyota and pulled the seat back so Tembo's mother could get out. Tembo had gotten out on his side, and I thought he would help her out of the vehicle; instead he just stood there and did not seem to know what to do. I saw she was having trouble getting out by herself, but she managed to get her head out of the door. I walked over to her and put my arm around her waist and lifted her out. Most of the Africans had never seen a white man do anything like this before. The "oohs" and "aahs" came from the crowd that had gathered around, and a smile came over Tembo's face. Immediately everyone started to shake my hand. Africans in the villages, in a gesture of friendship, shake hands like most people in the Western world, but they add something to it. This handshake is done in the usual manner, but then the palm of the hand is slipped up around the thumb of the other person and is repeated by both people. I tried several times but was not able to find out exactly what this gesture meant.

By now it had become dark and I had to turn on the Toyota lights. I told Tembo that we should get started home but I would like to return sometime to see his village people dance. This was all that was needed to get them started. Out came the homemade beer and the women started chanting and dancing in a circle in front of the headlights. They did not use a drum but kept time by clapping their hands. Only one or two women would dance at a time in the middle of the ring. The clapping was accompanied by a chant consisting of only three or four words repeated over and over. Tembo said the words simply meant, "we are dancing." The dancing lasted about fifteen minutes, and I saw that I would not get away very soon. The men did not take part in the dancing, only the women and a few children. Men have their own dances and do not dance with or at the same time as women.

Tembo's mother had by now seen that I was anxious to get away, so she broke up the dancing and brought me a chicken. His mother-in-law did the same thing. On the spur of the moment I thought I would show them how easy it was to put a chicken to sleep. I told Tembo that I could take any chicken and make it lie perfectly still on the ground when I walked away. He of course laughed and wanted to see this magic. Some children brought me another chicken that reacted quite wild. I took its head and tucked it under its wing, turned it over on its back, put it on the ground, and held the wings together with my hand. In about a minute I slowly took my hand off and the chicken did not move. Everyone had become very quiet at this, and I could see their eyes staring at the chicken. I let it stay that way for about twenty seconds, and then I shoved it over with my foot. The chicken jumped up squawking and ran away. At this people laughed and clapped their hands, and I got in the Toyota with Tembo and drove home. We were very late in getting back to Fort Jameson, and this day just reminded me that in Africa time is something that rural Africans don't worry about.

Working in Zambia just after Independence sometimes was very difficult because, as a white foreigner, I was automatically considered to be an expatriate, and sometimes this caused problems. The day after returning from Malawi I stopped at the local African open market to buy some vegetables before I went home. I had bought some tomatoes, carrots, and ground nuts when an African came up to me and asked to see my UNIP identification. I told the man that I worked for the United Nations and was exempt from belonging to political parties of the country where I worked. He, of course, did not even know what the United Nations was and said that a UNIP card was required to buy at the market. I started to walk away, but he still tried to sell me a card and finally said that he would see that I could not buy at the market on Saturday.

As the discussion was in progress, several Africans had started to gather around, and I thought this could turn into a bad situation. Although I had already paid for the tomatoes I laid them back on the table and walked away and immediately went to my office to write a letter the provincial minister. Two days later I received a reply from Minister Mbewe. He apologized for the trouble at the market and said he would take steps to see that it did not happen again.

When Saturday came I took Doris and went to the market as usual and the district secretary was there as well as the police. Evidently several other people had been stopped during the week and told that they could not buy vegetables at the market on Saturday. I had been the only one to write Minister Mbewe. While walking around the market, out of the corner of my eye I saw Joshua standing off away from the crowd as though he was deliberately trying to be inconspicuous. I played the game and did not look his way while shopping. The district secretary said my letter had given him the excuse to tell the minister that many complaints had been reported to him during the week. However mine had been the only one that would mean anything because I was a U.N. employee and a foreign diplomat.

I later had the opportunity to talk to the minister and explain that I had not written to him for an apology. My intention was to try to prevent any trouble that could lead to violence. One party really dominates the country, and intimidation goes on against people who do not want to be a member. One of the favorite pastimes of UNIP members was to turn people, especially whites, in to the government for slandering the president. The party was encouraging their youth to participate in political activities, and they formed an organization known as UNIP Youth. Since Joshua Njovo was active in UNIP, and because of his age, I thought he probably belonged to the youth organization, and this was something I planned to ask him about.

I arrived at the office early on Monday and was working on the aerial photographs when Joshua arrived. "Joshua, were you at the market on Saturday?" I asked.

"No, but I heard about your problem from some of my friends," he replied. "I told them that I worked for you and that you were not like the other white people in Fort Jameson and that they should not bother you to become a UNIP member," he said.

"I know that you belong to UNIP and attend most of their meetings, but are you a member of the youth organization?" I asked.

"No, I only participate as a member, not the Youth part because I do not have the time for both," he said.

I told Joshua that it was good that he was interested in his government and that being involved with his political party was part of the learning process in being a responsible citizen. The fact that he lied about not being at the market was a matter of concern, and I knew that I would have to be careful in what I did and said in his presence.

Work on the Luangwa Survey progressed very well, especially after the second team member arrived and I was able to concentrate on specific survey topics rather than on getting housing, licenses, the office set up, people hired, and equipment purchased and worrying about transportation. Now I was able to spend time on accumulating information from ongoing government projects, foreign-sponsored research, and my own observations, plus a lot of historical documents that were made available through government departments.

Field trips to various parts of the reserves to photograph conditions before and after the rainy season helped to put the natural cycle in perspective and how resources were affected. Of great value were the 1930 aerial photographs that, when compared to the 1965 photographs, told a story of vegetation change and erosion from well-used game trails. With the analysis and writing part of the report on a timely schedule, I was able to spend time tracking the activities of Chifungwe from information coming in from the field and my own flights over the Valley.

Pat came into my office and said that there was a car coming up the drive to the office that she recognized as belonging to Brian Compton. She quickly said that he was a strong opponent of the Game Department policies and that he probably just wanted to vent his views but that he was not a real threat to the project or the Department. He drove the car all the way up to my door, got out, and without hesitating walked into my office.

"My name is Brian Compton, and I represent the Friends of Luangwa Wildlife."

This was a little bit of a shock because I had not heard of or been told that such an organization existed in the Fort Jameson area. He came directly to the point by lecturing me for five minutes without stopping.

"It is people like you in FAO and employees of the Game Department that are spreading false information so that you will have a project to work on," he said.

"Employees in the government have the proper background and can solve all of the country's problems without outside help.

"You people just come here for several months to have a vacation and then leave without accomplishing anything," he continued.

"My reconnaissance trips to the game reserves indicate that there is no over abundance of animals and that they are not damaging the soil or vegetation. Use of vegetation by animals is natural and has been going on for hundreds of years, yet the animals are still there and the vegetation is still there," he said.

When Brian finally got to a place where he had to allow me to say something, I simply said: "Brian, I am sorry you feel this way because if higher levels of government felt that they had employees capable of doing the work, then I would not have to be here."

He seemed just as surprised about me making so bold a statement as I was about finding out about his organization. I thought that since he probably did not have any useful information that it would be best for me to ask him to leave—and I did. He left without saying another word, and I was glad to see him go.

As soon as Brian left, Pat walked across the veranda to my office and said, "You handled him very well, and you probably will not hear from him again. He does not have a formal college education and is a colonial holdover who worked as a records clerk for the Agricultural Department," she said.

Later I found out from Stan Stenton that the Friends of Luangwa Wildlife consisted of fewer than ten people total membership. He had not told me about them because they were considered more a pain than a problem.

Chapter Twelve

Stories were being told about an elephant in the Munyamadzi Corridor that had magical powers, and its left ear had a red glow in the evening hours. Game Guards began to get information from local villagers that the elephant with the glowing ear was an ancestor that came back in the form of an elephant and had the powers of a witch doctor. All one had to do was to get close enough to see the red ear from the front because the elephant had to look at your eyes so that he could project power to you to solve your problems. The word spreads fast in the bush, and tales often get changed when passed from one village to another, and the power of Chifungwe increased with each telling.

Laston Matshigi was a local hunter who lived in Kazembe village and had seen the red-eared elephant several times during and after the rainy season. He said he had heard about the animal from his cousins in the Game Department when they asked him to report his sightings when he was out in the corridor. The cousins knew that Laston was engaged in poaching, but they ignored his activities since many of their relatives depended on the product of his success. In the fall, before the rains started, Laston had observed three Game Department officials shoot this elephant with some type of small poisoned silver arrow that stuck in the elephant's skin, and he later went down on his side and died.

These men did strange things to the dead animal. They didn't cut out his ivory, cut off any parts, or take any meat. Instead they put their hands on him in many places and put this red thing in his ear. When they were through, one man stuck his hand on the elephant's ear, and in a few minutes he became alive again. The men returned to their vehicle and drove off but not out of sight of the animal. Laston stayed hidden in the bush where he could watch both the elephant and three men. The Game Department vehicle stayed there all night, but the red-eared elephant moved away in the early morning hours and Laston followed after him at a distance. In the following months Laston was able to use his knowledge of the marked elephant by telling villagers in the corridor that it had special powers and that he could lead them to the "gray ghost" to ask for healing or grant special requests.

Chifungwe traveled through the corridor with other elephants, creating havoc in many gardens. In prior years, when elephant depredation had been particularly bad, the government had to bring in food by lorry to keep the people in the corridor from dying of starvation. During these periods the Game Department had assisted by providing meat from their cropping station and from elephant control.

I had accumulated enough information from aerial observations and on-the-ground sightings to establish a movement pattern for Chifungwe. His day-to-day movements could cover a large area, but he seemed to go with the seasons because of the availability of food. His general mode of behavior was to travel outside the reserve at night into the corridor and the gardens until morning when he returned to the reserve protected area. In the rainy season he was all over the place exploring territory from the Muchinga escarpment to the center of the South Reserve and to Nsefu and Luambe. When it was dry his travels were along the river areas in the Munyamadzi Corridor but only infrequently into the game reserves.

Chifungwe used the Munyamadzi Corridor more than any other place in the Luangwa Valley. It extends from the base of the Muchinga escarpment to the Luangwa River for most of the distance between the present South and North Luangwa Game Reserves. The corridor is an area of approximately 800 square miles, heavily tsetse fly-infested, and with daily temperatures in October and November often hitting 115 degrees Fahrenheit.

Because Number 33 would roam in the general area of the corridor, I wanted to learn more about the history of the area. I made an in-depth review of reports by researchers who had worked in the area, obtained information from annual reports by the Game Department, located and studied past and recent aerial photographs, made numerous field trips through the area, and from published literature studied the history of the people.

Residents in the corridor are Bisa who came from the Congo at the same time as the Bemba tribe about 1630. The Bemba have a highly structured society and did a lot of trade with the Arabs. In the 1820s and '30s conflicts occurred between the Bemba and Bisa to the south, eventually splitting the Bisa, who moved into the Bangweulu Swamps and Luangwa Valley areas. Hunting with muzzleloaders in the Munyamadzi Corridor is practiced with considerable success by the Bisa. Although the full-time hunter is uncommon, a few people kill game and distribute meat according to their lineage, receiving maize and other plant foods in return from local growers. Such a hunter becomes a meat provider through clan relationships and inheritance.

Hunting and the kill are ritualized, and the perceived relationship between the hunter, his ancestors, and the animal becomes a strong influence in the future success of the hunter. The vast majority of male residents hunt in their spare time, and these people account for the greater number of animals killed. Children sometimes hunt and use catapults to kill small birds, which often find their way into the relish pot. The Game and Fish Department allows a specific number of animals to be killed on license by villagers in the corridor. In all likelihood, the actual number killed exceeds the number authorized.

The Bisa have a color scheme of white, black, and red. A ritual connotation of certain colors and color combinations determine their selection or non-selection of birds and mammals. They regard creatures of these colors in the natural world as placed by God to remind them of the symbolic meaning of the colors. These colors are used consistently and repeatedly in their rituals. Black is witchcraft; white is purity, health, and strength; while red symbolizes human or other animal blood. Hunting medicines are composed primarily of red and white substances. When I ordered it, I had no way of knowing, and it did not occur to me that the tag in Chifungwe's ear might make him a desirable animal to kill because of its red and white colors.

The soil adjacent to the Munyamadzi River is very rich and capable of growing two crops a year in sorghum, maize, and groundnuts. The river is the watering place of a large game population in the backcountry around the escarpment, but to reach the water they have to go through cultivated areas. It is not only during the dry season that damage occurs. Although there is a more random dispersal of elephants during the rains, they are still present in riverine areas when the rainy season crops are growing. At the beginning of the rains many elephant move purposely to garden areas, including those of the corridor. While the elephant is the major culprit most often complained about, buffalo and hippo not only eat the vegetation but also trample plants and churn up the soil.

Over a period of six months I flew over the Chifungwe Plain and Munyamadzi Corridor many times and made several three- to four-day expeditions by vehicle and on foot. The importance of elephants and their use of the area became clear as I completed aerial counts of the Chifungwe and Pande Plains. The Chifungwe had a density of eighteen elephants per square mile and Pande Plain thirty-three per square mile. All the field huts and houses in and around the crops have gongs and other devices for frightening animals away from gardens. Considering that one elephant eats several hundred pounds of forage a day, the damage to crops from a family group or herd can be devastating and a great loss to the villager.

It is the policy of the Game Department to kill marauding elephants, and many are killed on garden control operations each year in the corridor. The Bisa consider this a service and are overjoyed when an elephant is killed since the meat goes to them. The government takes the ivory and tail. Still, the feeling of the villagers toward elephants is one of ambivalence. They would rather be free to kill the elephant themselves, in numbers they choose and at times they please. As long as the Bisa people exist in the corridor, conflicts will continue and probably will increase.

One of my plans had been to schedule a trip to the Munyamadzi Corridor to take my family to visit Stuart and Martha Marks. Stuart was a Ford Foundation Scholar doing research for his doctorate degree and had lived in Nabwalya for almost a year. Stuart had provided information for our Luangwa report and many times had asked me to bring the family to stay all night in the village. I needed a break from a hectic schedule so made arrangements with him to visit for a few days.

We got up at 5:30 on a Saturday morning, had breakfast, and left for the Luangwa Valley. By previous arrangement Stuart was to meet us at the river crossing at the Chibemba pontoon. We arrived at 9:15 and found an African waiting for us with a note from Stuart. He was at the first village across the river interviewing a headman. The African was named "Happy," and he showed me the way to the village. At this time of the year, just after the rains, the roads are very difficult to find because of high vegetation, and Happy was a welcome addition to our already loaded Toyota.

I saw Stuart's Land Rover and pulled up near it in the village. Villagers wanting to shake hands with Doris and the girls immediately surrounded us. They crowded around the car so much that Stuart had to come to rescue us and ask them to move away. The women were especially attracted to Doris and Myra because of their light complexions and long blond hair. I expect for some of them Myra was the first white child with blond hair they had seen.

We finally got away from the village and drove on toward Nabwalya. Stuart stopped at another village to let off a rider, and I got a chance to see a village store. Doris and the girls stayed in the Toyota, and several children came to talk to them. The store was a round hut about ten feet in diameter and had a chest-high bamboo counter. The contents consisted of one homemade dress, half a box of batteries, salt, razor blades, and several bolts of cloth. Several cans of food were on the back shelf, but it was too dark to see what they were. I was anxious to see if there were any Cokes for sale. There was an old wooden case with four Cokes left, and all were covered with dust. Coca-Cola usually can be found even in the remotest of places. Warm Cokes are quite good once one gets used to them, but by now they were a real treat for us.

While I was in the store, some children brought Doris baobab fruit to eat. The gourd-like fruit has to be cracked open to get a tart, chalky substance, and it is very high in Vitamin C.

We started off again for Nabwalya and only stopped twice more, once to admire an unusually large buffalo and again for Stuart to shoot several guinea fowl. Martha was waiting for us when we arrived. The first thing we did was to wash off about an inch of dust. We had brought some fresh tomatoes, so canned lunchmeat with tomatoes, peaches for dessert, and orange Crush to drink was the medicine for our hunger pangs.

Visitors for the next few hours were many. As in the village where we had stopped earlier, the African women seemed to be fascinated by Myra and wanted to touch her hair, and all of them had to shake Doris's hand. These villagers appeared to me to be quite different from those who migrated to the towns and cities. They were polite and seemed to bubble over with happiness. Their needs were simple, and they lived off the land without much help from the government.

It soon got dark and Stuart asked me to go with him to meet Chief Nabwalya. We found him outside his house sitting on a small stool in front of the fire. He had his leg stretched out because his foot was swollen and evidently very painful. He had had this condition for several years, but it had been getting worse the past couple of months. It is difficult for a doctor to make a diagnosis on an African that lives in the bush. Generally it is not one problem but several that cause the medical problem. Stuart told me that the chief had forty-three wives scattered around the Valley. I figured anyone who could put up with that many women could not be too sick.

We arrived back at our hut about 8:00 P.M., and Stuart asked me if I wanted to have some fun killing mice. I had noticed that the grass rustled a lot, and every few minutes I would get a glimpse of mice running between grass bunches. Three of us—Stuart; Dyson, his assistant; and me—armed ourselves with a club and flashlight and took off mice hunting in an abandoned hut. The mice were running all over the place, and I have never seen so many at once in my life. We were swatting at them in all directions as they were running around our feet. The battle moved outside and took on new dimensions. Others in the village were also out on this community rat patrol. I was laughing so hard at Stuart, Dyson, and the villagers that I had to quit and just watch the action.

When we went to bed that night the mice were so numerous in our hut, running on the ground floor, over our bed, and falling from the thatch overhead that Doris and I had to get up and go outside. We had made beds in the Toyota for the girls, so they were not bothered. Stuart and Martha could not sleep either, so we built a fire to heat water for tea. Stuart said Dyson would think that we were witches because only witches got up at this hour and built a fire. The night was long, but morning finally arrived and we had to get ready to return to Fort Jameson. After breakfast we said goodbye to the villagers and started off for town. Stuart and Martha drove part of the way back in their Land Rover just to make certain we stayed on the right track. As we left, the children were all running along with the Toyota and waving until we got past the village. This was certainly one of our most enjoyable trips to a rural area in Zambia and one that we would not forget.

Chapter Thirteen

A runner notified Stan Stenton that both of us were to come to the government complex and to the minister's office as soon as possible. I was in my office working on the analysis of my aerial survey data when Stan arrived. He did not look too happy, but I greeted him anyway, asking, "What is wrong? You look concerned."

"Minister Mbewe has requested our presence in his office right away," he said. "This is unusual because he knows that you are a United Nations employee. I know that he wants your efforts to succeed because it will look good on his record that the UN funded a development project in his province. I have no idea what he wants, especially since it includes you."

I climbed into Stan's Land Rover and went with him to the government offices. Minister Mbewe was on the telephone talking to someone in Lusaka, and I heard him say, "They are here now."

He walked to the entrance of his office and motioned for us to come in. This was about the fifth time that I had actually visited with the minister, and he was becoming more accustomed to me and we seemed to get along fine. On one visit when I was explaining what the outcome of our survey would likely be, he asked me a lot of questions about Washington, D.C. He became even more interested when he found out that I had lived and worked there for the government. It was not until a later chance meeting that he told me he was being considered for an appointment to the Zambian Embassy in Washington.

"I was just on the telephone to Government House in Lusaka talking to the Minister of Parks and Tourism. He was quite upset because word has come to him from the Munyamadzi Corridor, and in particular from Chief

Nabwalya, that elephants are destroying not just crops but also huts and grain storage bins as they escape from the gardens and he wants the Game Department to initiate elephant control. The Chief told him that a young male that seems to have some power over the other elephants leads the raids."

While smiling, he said, "Now what is this nonsense about an elephant with a glowing red ear in the Munyamadzi Corridor?"

I explained the capturing and marking process and what the data from knowing the movements of Chifungwe would mean in determining park boundaries. While he sympathized with us about the need for information, he also explained that he had an obligation to protect the villagers and their food source and that some elephants would have to be killed. He also thought that the one with the red ear had to be included because it was stirring up the emotions of too many villagers.

At this point I had to think about our survey goals and whether this one animal had already made his contribution. I asked the minister if he would excuse us for a few minutes to go outside and talk. We walked outside the building and stood in the shade of a jacaranda tree.

"Stan, what is your feeling about his request for the Department to kill elephants in the corridor?" I asked.

"As far as the Department is concerned, his word is law and so is his request," he said. "He has complete control over the Eastern Province, and government employees have to respond to his authority even though we do not work for him directly. At this point in time killing ten to fifteen elephants on two or three patrols is not going to do anything to the population and it is politically acceptable," Stan said.

"We have already collected a lot of information from this animal.

"What if you go ahead with the control effort now but let Chifungwe alone and I will try to capture him again to remove the ear tag?" I asked. "I feel obligated to Number 33 to try to save his life since I am the one that caused his trouble when he became a celebrity. Without the ear tag he would not be considered the leader of the herd," I said.

"Mbewe does not have to know that he will not be shot on the first control operation but only that you will carry out his request.

"All I ask for is a week to remove the ear tag after you have completed the first control operation. If I am successful then the elephant with the red ear will not be seen again. If I am not successful then you will be free to kill him on the next control operation. Is this agreeable to you?" I asked.

"This sounds like a good plan, so let's go tell Mbewe," he said. We went back into the office and the minister looked up from his desk.

"David has suggested that he has enough information from the marked elephant, and we can go ahead and initiate the first control operation within the next few days. You can let the Minister in Government House know that you have solved the problem," Stan said.

"I really appreciate your help in this matter, and if I can help either of you in any way in the future, you can come to me directly," Mbewe said. With that said we excused ourselves and walked outside, got into the Land Rover, and drove to the Colonial House to have a Castle beer.

The next day Stan gave instructions to his Game Guards to start the elephant control operation just south of Nabwalya where the elephants cross the Mupamadzi River coming out of the South Reserve.

"If the elephant with the red ear is among the group, he will be allowed to escape," he told the Guards. "We will take care of him in another way.

"If one of you shoots this elephant, you will lose your job with the Game Department and be sent back to your village, so pay careful attention to the left ear of what you intend to shoot." The control operation involved four Game Guards with orders to shoot up to ten animals on this first effort. The only items that the villagers would not be allowed to keep were the tusks and tail.

While the Game Department was initiating the control process, I was trying to contact Robert Lawson to schedule a flight. Ian had left the Game Department several days earlier to be on his way to the U.S. to start his college program. On this trip to find Chifungwe, it would be Sam, James, and me on the ground and Robert Lawson in the air. Our plan was to drive to the Plains area the first day and to start the search the second day. Robert would go in the air each day and make radio contact with us on the ground to determine our progress. He would fly the area back and forth until he spotted our animal.

I returned to my office from the meeting with the minister and had been there for about an hour when Douglas DeGroot pulled up in his Land Rover. I knew something was wrong because Douglas usually did not spend much time at the headquarters in Fort Jameson. His parents originally were from The Netherlands, but he was born in the bush in South Africa and preferred living in rural areas where there were not many humans. Douglas was a Game Ranger assigned to animal control and worked out of the Luangwa Command but made trips to all the other reserves when his expertise was required. The Game Department had a policy that rangers could not go by themselves on a control situation that involved dangerous animals, and that is why he came to see me.

"This morning there was a child killed by a leopard and was dragged into the bush just outside of the Nsefu Reserve," he said "All of the Game Guards and other rangers are gone, and Stan has left for Mfuwe. I need you to go with me to track down the leopard and be my backup. I know you can handle a rifle as well as anyone in the Department, but if you do not want to go I will understand. While there is some danger involved, the leopard has already fed and will not be so aggressive, and we have a good chance of getting him if we get underway soon."

"It is a job that I do not particularly like, but it is also important for your safety that you not go alone, so I will do it," I said to Douglas.

"I really appreciate your help on this; we will go by the office, and I will check out a .375 rifle for you."

We arrived at the village outside of Nsefu, and the inhabitants gathered around the Rover rather quickly, demanding that Douglas go after and kill the leopard. He spent several minutes assuring the villagers that we were there to track it down and shoot it on sight. The parents of the four-year-old boy took us to their hut and showed us the blood trail leading away from the village.

Douglas would take the lead in following the trail, and I would stay about ten feet behind with a cartridge in the chamber and the safety off. The trail was obvious. Marked by blood and displaced litter, we only had to follow it about half a mile in an area that was in fairly open but clumpy vegetation.

Visibility was good, and it did not take long to spot our query resting under a tree beside what was left of the remains of the child. The leopard had not spotted us and did not move. Douglas whispered that he wanted to ease closer to get a clear shot at the heart, and we walked forward slowly while keeping trees between us and the leopard. When we got to within thirty yards, Douglas, with his rifle ready to shoulder, stepped to the right of the trees. As he did the leopard got up on all fours and looked in our direction; at that instant Douglas fired.

We saw the leopard go down, and it did not move. Douglas said that we would stay here for several minutes to make certain that he remained still. Since the animal did not move we walked around behind the tree and approached it from the back. The bullet had entered the heart and there was considerable blood where it had exited. For certain he was dead, and Douglas walked around to the front side and said that it was okay to come forward. What was left of the child was not recognizable, and Douglas had anticipated this. He had brought a piece of canvas in his kit to wrap around the body before taking the remains back to the village. The leopard turned out to be a female and had a lower jaw that was deformed in front. There was only a stump of a canine at the gum line and no incisors. This animal would have had difficulty taking any antelope species, and that was probably why it attacked and killed a child.

We went back to the village to get the Land Rover and were met by a crowd of villagers. They had heard the shot and assumed that the leopard was dead. The parents asked about the child, but they knew that his body would not be all there. We told them that we wrapped his remains in a cloth cover and would bring him back to them along with the leopard so they could see that it was actually dead. We drove back to the kill site and loaded the leopard into the Land Rover first and then laid the canvas with the body on top. When we arrived it seemed like everyone from this village and some from other villages as well had gathered to receive the body and to look at the leopard. Douglas thought it was not a good idea to linger since the crowd was large and many of them were pushing and shoving to get to the leopard to touch its body.

After removing the canvas and giving it to the parents, Douglas told them he had to take the leopard to the Game Department, so we got back into the Land Rover and started to slowly pull away. It was obvious that many more people wanted to see the animal, but we finally got through the crowd and were on our way back to Fort Jameson. Douglas said that this was not his first time in killing an animal that had killed a human and added "It is especially difficult if the victim was a child because parents tend to go into a crazy emotional state, and it is not safe to be around them when this happens."

We arrived back in Fort Jameson late in the evening, and several Game Guards had returned from the field. Douglas turned the leopard over to two guards to skin and dispose of the carcass, except that I asked for them to clean the meat off the head and save the skull for me to examine and later to put into their museum in Lusaka. The skin would be dried and put into storage in the warehouse for sale at a later date.

Chapter Fourteen

Now that the decision had been made to remove the red tag from Chifungwe's ear, our next task would be to locate him from the air and to guide a crew to the same location on the ground. There was a good chance that he could be found in the plains area or between the Munyamadzi and Mupamadzi Rivers, and this is the area that we would search first. I contacted Robert and asked him to be prepared to fly the game reserves and corridor on consecutive days for a week. He did not know about the meeting with the Minister and wanted to know why the intense schedule. After I explained the situation he was saddened that we would have to stop an effort that was continuing to be successful and that he had helped establish. However, he understood the reason, and he wanted to assist in the effort of giving Chifungwe a chance to live. We agreed that he would start early each day and fly with a Game Department observer from Mpika in all the areas that we knew to be places that our elephant frequented.

The plan was simple. Sam, James, and I would be camped north of the Munyamadzi River so that we could make radio contact with Robert flying the observation plane. We would have to be prepared for living in the bush for a stay of up to seven days—the limit of time that we had to find Chifungwe. From our camp location we could easily move toward the escarpment or around the corridor. Robert would have a handheld radio in the Cessna, and we would have another unit in the Land Rover.

I left Fort Jameson on Sunday morning loaded with camping equipment that I borrowed from the Game Department and food that I bought from

Jasat's store. James and Sam were waiting for me at Mfuwe with their kits and rifles, and I picked them up there.

We decided to go as far as the Mutinondo River to stay the first night. I had flown over this area several times and had seen the Mutinondo Falls with water coming out of the escarpment close to the top. The Mutinondo River was a clear stream free of the usual diseases and was known for having tiger fish. Stan had told me about this fish and that I should try my luck when I had the chance.

Since we arrived and selected a suitable campsite before dinnertime, I took my spinning rod and started walking the stream and casting a lure in the fast water. The tiger fish has very sharp teeth and I had to use a steel leader because this fish could easily cut through a regular fishing line. I was walking along the edge of the stream under a bank that was about seven feet in height.

I had been doing this for about thirty minutes while all the time watching the water for the silver-colored fish to hit the lure when I caught the distinct odor of an elephant and had the uncomfortable feeling of not being alone. There was nothing in front or to the back of me, and I looked up on the bank ahead and to my left—there was an elephant with his trunk in a tree and standing very close to the edge. I sort of froze for a minute and then realized that he did not know that I was there, and I slowly started to back away to get around a curve where I could not be seen. Once around the curve I turned around and retraced my original path to the river and got well away from the elephant.

When I got back to camp I told James and Sam about my encounter, and they sort of scolded me for not being aware of where I was and not watching my surroundings. Sam told me that I was probably safe because elephants do not like to come down steep banks, but this was not a guarantee.

The night went without incident, and at about 8:30 I heard Robert's plane coming up the valley along the escarpment. I turned on the radio and made contact and asked him to fly a pattern using the escarpment as his baseline. I would leave the radio on in case he spotted our animal. This type of search went on for five days and we had moved our campsite two times.

It was Saturday morning when I heard the noise of the plane coming up along the escarpment to the west. Robert had crossed over the top further down than on previous mornings and just crossed over the Munyamadzi when he made contact.

"David this is Robert. Do you copy?"

"I copy, Robert."

"I am just north of the reserve boundary. Let's go to air frequency," he said.

"Okay, I have switched; why the need for ground silence?" I asked.

"My contacts in Mpika tell me that railroad workers from other countries have portable radios, and some of them have gotten into the hands of poachers. There is a Land Rover about three miles away that seems to be searching for something, and my guess is that it is Chifungwe. I now have your animal in sight and do not want to give away his location. When the driver hears my plane he most likely will tune his radio to your ground frequency. My observer has the vehicle in his binoculars. There are four people in the Land Rover which is not too far from Chifungwe. Please advise."

"Fly over their vehicle to let them see you. Let me know if they change direction. Our location is just north of Pande Plain tracking through the bush," I said.

"The vehicle is turning off the track and appears to be making a circle and heading east," Robert said.

"The anti-poaching unit is not in the corridor today, so we are the only people from the Game Department in this area," I replied. "They probably do not know that we are here.

"I have a fix on the Muchinga escarpment with the Cessna in the direct line of sight. We will continue toward the escarpment."

"What is our animal doing?" I asked Robert.

"He appears to be just resting," he replied. "What's your desire?" he asked.

"Fly low over the vehicle several times. Have your observer take photographs of the vehicle and then head back to Mfuwe. Batteries in our handheld radio are about dead and all our backup batteries are now drained, so contact may not be possible again after you leave. Let Johnny Uys at Mwfue know our circumstances," I told Robert.

For the next hour we drove slowly through the mopane vegetation, missing trees, and large rocks, but not the low brush that sometimes scraped the bottom of the Land Rover and got caught in the fan belt. All of our capture equipment was ready. The dart was loaded with M99. For safety purposes the dart was not in the gun's chamber but packed inside a leather case. If it went off accidentally the serum would eject harmlessly into the case.

Getting the permit to use drugs for capturing animals was not a simple matter through legal channels. It involved getting a potent substance that had to be brought in from the U.K., and this included a risk that the drug would get into the wrong hands. Because of the bureaucracy involved, I had made arrangements to get M99 from an FAO biologist in Malawi who could easily get the drug from the pharmaceutical company because they had an outlet in that country, but this was done without the approval of the government and involved considerable risk. Earlier I had made arrangements to meet him at the border to deliver some drugs that I had ordered several months ago. About a mile from the border I was stopped by uniformed military troops carrying automatic weapons.

The sergeant in charge asked me to get out of the vehicle and wanted to see my identification papers. While he was examining my Laissez Passer and talking to me, his men were taking everything out of the Toyota and checking each item very carefully. Unfortunately I had my capture gun and equipment in the Toyota because of getting ready for the trip to Luangwa, but the drugs were locked in a safe in my office back in Fort Jameson. Weapons in Zambia were strictly controlled, and the sergeant was starting to get suspicious. He looked at the Palmer capture gun and dart and noticed that it was different and I did not have any shells that matched the large shotgun chamber.

I showed him an empty dart, how it loaded, and explained that it worked like a hypodermic needle for giving shots to humans. He understood this but wanted to know what I was going to do with the gun. I went through a lengthy explanation of what I was doing in Zambia and how the gun would be used. He wanted to know how it fired and what I used as a shell. I had a dummy practice dart and the thought occurred to me that if I let him fire the gun with a dart he would allow me to proceed. I showed him a CO_2 cartridge that I loaded in the power tube and then placed the dummy dart in the chamber. I walked about twenty yards and set a cardboard box from my Toyota in the road. By now his troops were starting to watch more intently. I asked him if he was a good marksman, and of course the answer was obvious.

Intentionally I did not tell him that the dart would not go straight as the bullet came from a rifle, and I knew at twenty yards he would not hit the center of the box. He put the butt of the gun to his shoulder and pointed it at the box and fired. He was expecting a recoil as with a regular gun, but this did not happen and he flinched at the *poof* made by the capture gun instead of the crack of a cartridge from a rifle. The dart landed in the ground in front of the box and the soldiers laughed. He handed my Laissez Passer back to me and said that I could proceed.

As he gave me the document he asked where I was going and when I would return. "Only to the border to meet a biologist from Malawi," I said. All the while he was eyeing six bottles of Castle beer that had been removed from the back of my Toyota. I had already learned that small tokens of friendship and gifts often get results far more valuable than the gift. I asked, "Do you like beer?"

"It is my favorite drink," he said.

I gave him the beer and told him that I hoped to see him again. He told the soldiers to replace the items in my Toyota and that I could proceed. Later I found out that the search was for insulin that was being smuggled across the border from Zambia to Malawi for a political opponent of the current president of Malawi.

As we continued our search for Chifungwe and progressed northwest, the tree density decreased and we could now see a quarter mile through the vegetation. We had to work our way around several small family groups of elephants and some large herds of buffalo that regularly move back and forth between the open plains, mopane, and riverine vegetation between the North and South Luangwa Reserves. It is an area that also has some of the largest buffalo herds in East Africa. Contrary to popular belief, buffalo will move away when encountering a vehicle, but this is a herd characteristic and does not pertain to females with calves or single males. I had already had a confrontation with a female and a calf and was aware of the dangers.

While driving in the South Reserve on a reconnaissance trip, a female buffalo and calf were crossing the road about ten yards in front of my Toyota. She stopped for a minute, turned her head, looked at the vehicle, and immediately charged toward the front of the Land Rover and ran directly into the radiator. She shook her head as if to gain consciousness and then went back to her calf and crossed the road. Fortunately the vehicle had several steel bars across the front and there was no damage. After the incident I often thought about what would have happened if I had been outside of the vehicle when she made the charge.

We made every effort to avoid large mammal species and concentrated our effort on our fixed point on the escarpment in trying to find one single male elephant that had become a legend in the Munyamadzi Corridor and Luangwa Valley and therefore a trophy animal and a target for poachers. Without our air support helping in the search it was slow travel, but we did not want the plane to linger in the area to draw attention to the ground activity.

At this time of year the low woody vegetation and grasses were getting dry and hot and tsetse flies were abundant. It was not too difficult to create our own vehicle track. This was much better than during wet times when the rains made the cotton soil slick as ice with only a little moisture present. We had been away from Fort Jameson for five days and were starting to run low on food, water, and fuel—not to mention the fact that the three of us were getting physically tired and really needed a break. James and Sam were starting to get on my nerves and my temper was just a little too short. However, these two companions were very tolerant and forgiving, and I trusted them with my life, but as yet I did not have the bush experience for them to have the same feeling. I had already made the decision that if we could not find our target animal within the next few hours we would make camp for the night and start for Mfuwe in the morning.

We probably had about three hours left before dark, which comes early in areas close to the equator, and I was dreading the thought of running out of time for us and for Chifungwe. I was also anxious about the animal's well-being and did not want to inadvertently draw attention to his general location. After about an hour we were nearing the Mupamadzi River when Sam patted me on the shoulder with his left hand and pointed to a rear-end scratching against a mopane tree. We could see the back of the left ear and I would have to slowly circle around to get a look at the front to see if he had the "thing" attached. His location was near that reported by Robert based on our line of travel to the Muchinga fixed point, and we had gone about the right distance. We hoped that our target animal was the one we were seeing.

I had to make a decision of stopping now about fifty yards away and behind the animal and risk that he was not our target or to continue to go ahead with the chance that he would move off and we would not have time to pursue him further. James stopped the vehicle and the three of us got out. I chose to take the capture gun and Sam with a .375 rifle for security, move slowly to twenty yards behind the animal, and then walk slowly ahead to where I could see the front of his ear. Fortunately he just then laid both ears back against his body and I did not have to move a step further. There it was, the "gray ghost" of Chifungwe with his ten-inch diameter red-and-white ear tag with the number 33 that I put there eight months previously.

My heart was pumping adrenalin; my hands were sweaty and not as steady as usual. All I could think of was getting the dart loaded into the capture gun quieter than I had ever done before. I draped a folded towel loosely around the closed bolt and my hand to deaden the sound, opened the chamber, put the dart in place, pushed the bolt into the barrel, locked the safety on, and removed the towel. Sam was ready with his .375 caliber H & H magnum rifle as a backup if the elephant charged. He positioned himself about two feet behind and to my right and had his rifle in the across-the-breast ready position. The huge gray rump presented a perfect target. I slowly raised the weapon that was just a remanufactured shotgun powered by carbon dioxide instead of a shell.

The adrenalin was still at work and I could feel the anxiety, but my hands were relaxed and now dry. I aimed a little high at a spot on a muscle knowing the dart would fall about six to eight inches over those twenty yards. Our target remained calm, unaware that we were nearby; there was no wind and not a cloud in the sky. I slowly eased off the safety, mentally reminding myself that there would not be a kickback, slowly pulled the trigger, and the gun fired with a loud *poof*. The dart found its mark, penetrated the skin into the muscle, and remained fixed. He flinched and hunched forward a few feet. What the elephant did next may have saved our lives.

Chifungwe turned completely around while extending his trunk upright in the air searching for an odor, he made a shrill trumpet—and then he charged. My hair stood on end and I froze. Time seemed to pass very slowly as Sam was raising his rifle and took aim. At first Chifungwe's thrust seemed to be in our direction and I could feel the dry ground shake, but he headed directly for two men about forty yards away who were running from behind nearby trees. The poachers had been caught completely by surprise; in a state of shock they dropped their weapons and radio and, as they grasped the danger, started running for their vehicle that had been concealed in dense vegetation.

The Tanzanian was much faster and quickly got ahead of the Zambian. Chifungwe was charging full force at them, but he was losing steam as the drug began to take effect more quickly because of his increased activity. He ran over one poacher, and although his gait began to slow, he continued to charge toward the other. With the engine still running and one door open, the Tanzanian was able to get inside the Land Rover. But while the Chinaman had been watching the Tanzanian running toward the vehicle, Laston had quietly jumped out and disappeared into the bush. We heard a door shut and the vehicle that had been hidden in the vegetation drove off crushing brush as it left. The frightened occupants were unaware that the elephant's speed seemed to lessen as the Land Rover lurched forward to escape the elephant's charge. Raising a great cloud of dust they rushed away leaving the Zambian behind.

Without our knowledge, these poachers had been following Chifungwe and had come within shooting range of us and of our elephant without us seeing them. We were moving through the bush at a cautious rate without disturbance and dust so that it was possible that another vehicle would not detect our presence and we did not detect theirs. After the aircraft left the area they had returned to the bush to locate Chifungwe. Because our radio was now dead we could not call for air support, and if we could have there was not sufficient time for them to respond while there was still light. Their radios had not been modified to include the Game Department frequencies, and they had not heard the discussion that had taken place between the aircraft and my marking crew.

The Zambian was not aware that, as a result of a schedule change after he left Fort Jameson, we were in the area stalking the same elephant as the poachers. We did not see the vehicle and were not able to identify the poacher who got inside, but as it left we saw the elephant had slowed to a walk and gradually went down, although still fighting and trying to continue the chase. We picked up the guns and radio dropped by the poachers, removed the batteries and put them in our own handheld unit, but we were not able to make contact with Mfuwe or the anti-poaching unit.

Since the poachers were armed, our assumption was that they would not have let us leave the site alive. By charging the poachers instead of us, Chifungwe certainly put the odds in our favor of surviving an encounter with the heavily armed poachers. To them the ivory and animal parts that they were after were worth more that the lives of three men.

Sam and I walked to where we thought our elephant had trampled one of the men. After several minutes of searching we found his body with his chest completely crushed. He was dead and the ground was soaked with blood. His face was turned to the side, but something was familiar about this person, and when I turned his head up I immediately recognized Joshua Njovo. All we could do at this point was to wrap the body in our tent and lay him in the back of the Land Rover. To do this we had to remove one back seat and turn it sideways so the body would fit without contorting into a grotesque shape.

While Sam remained on guard, I quickly went to work removing the ear tag from Chifungwe. Once this was done he would no longer be in danger.

Although he would have a hole in his ear, he would look just like any other elephant and the "gray ghost" would no longer exist. I had to have James hold a spanner on one side of the bolt that held the ear tag in place while I twisted the nut on the other side. The washer and nut combination had done its work well. It took several tries to finally move the first nut, but once the tension was relieved, the nut and washer came off easily. The hole in the ear was not much larger than when I made it with the leather punch, and the skin of the ear had developed a callus within the hole. Because I would not have a way to identify Chifungwe once the ear tag was gone I decided to paint a white spot on his back with rubberized paint that could be seen from the air. If the paint lasted only a week or so that would be long enough to check on his location and that he in fact was surviving. With the tag out there was no reason to keep the elephant down.

It would soon be completely dark, so we loaded all our gear in the Land Rover and James got into the driver's seat. He backed up to within ten feet of Chifungwe, and Sam got in the left side with his .375 still ready to use. I had already loaded a regular veterinary syringe with the M285 antidote. With the engine running and James ready to make a fast exit, I walked up to Number 33. I took the cloth patch off that I had laid over his exposed left eye. His eye was moist, and it seemed to have water coming from one corner. I laid my hand on the side of his face and hoped he could understand the message I wanted him to have: Survive, live to a ripe old age, and father many descendants. I put my knee on his side, lifted up his ear and inserted the needle in a large vein. The antidote works exceedingly fast, and I had to quickly put pressure on the plunger to get the entire drug in the blood. I withdrew the needle and jumped into the back of the Land Rover.

We pulled away to about twenty yards, and within two minutes Chifungwe was trying to get to his feet. By the end of four minutes he was up and shaking his head as though he had a big hangover, which I suspect he did. He turned in different directions as if he were deliberately searching for something to charge, although I doubt that a charge would have lasted very long. By now night was close at hand and we had to decide whether to stay where we were for the night to make certain that he was okay and to provide some protection if the poachers should happen to return. I also had to consider how long I could keep Joshua's body wrapped in canvas before it would start to give off a strong odor. I figured I had at least twenty-four hours before I needed to turn the body over to the Game Department at Mfuwe.

My decision was to move slowly around to the front to a point of about fifty yards away where we could see Chifungwe and also in the direction that the other vehicle had taken. The two poachers probably had already connected with the dirt track that runs east and south and would be across the river and out of the reserve before long. We had to assume that they had another radio and would contact other people to let them know their status and those who were returning home. We made no further attempts to contact Mfuwe by radio so as not to provide any information to the poachers in case they changed their minds and tried to return.

The night had a cloudless sky, and Chifungwe was still easy to see. Sam remained on guard while James and I made coffee and heated some corned beef and beans over our two single-burner camp stoves. The flame was small and could not be seen at a great distance, so we were safe from being spotted except for someone at very close range. Sam had lived in the bush most of his life and could hear and identify the night sounds. I knew that he would be able to warn us if anything was not natural.

The night passed without incident, and as the morning sky started to light the area, we could see that Chifungwe was gone. Sam said that he had starting slowly walking southwest in the direction of the Muchinga escarpment. To me this was a good sign because there were no regularly traveled roads or tracks in that direction. We drove back to Mfuwe and made contact with Johnny Uys to tell him what had happened. Robert had informed Johnny yesterday that we had observed poachers in the area where we had located Chifungwe. We explained the circumstances that led to the trampling of Joshua Njovo and that at least three other poachers had escaped. Johnny said that we should take the body directly to the police in Fort Jameson and that they would need a statement from me, Sam, and James.

"I will radio Stan to let him know you are coming with the body and for him to notify the police commissioner," Johnny said. "We work very closely with the police in Fort Jameson and Stan knows Commissioner Musonda very well and there will not be any problems. Since there were three witnesses to the death, it will be routine and just for the record. The police will take care of the body and notify relatives. However, since Joshua was involved with a poaching ring, the Game Department and police will investigate his connection." Johnny said.

At this point I remembered that Robert Lawson had his observer take a photograph of the vehicle, and from this the police could trace the license number if it were visible on the photograph. Robert had already returned to Mpika, and I told Johnny Uys that I would call Lawson as soon as I got back to Fort Jameson. I needed to talk to him anyway because I would like to fly along the escarpment within the next day or two to try to locate Chifungwe.

When we arrived at the police station at Fort Jameson, Commissioner Musonda was waiting for us.

"Dr. Patton, please drive to the morgue behind this building, and I will have two attendants remove the body," he said. "Stan Stenton called to let me know that you were coming and the circumstances involving the deceased person. All I need from you is a signed statement of what happened. List the two witnesses in your statement, but they do not have to write one of their own. Yours will be sufficient, and you can drop this off to me in the next few days.

"I understand that you may have a picture of the other three fellows and the number of their license plate. I hope the picture turns out to be good so that we can check on the ownership of the vehicle," Musonda said.

"We appreciate your help on this matter, Commissioner, and I will get copies of the photographs as soon a I can," I said.

I drove the Land Rover around to the morgue where the two assistants were waiting. They removed the body, which was now stiff, and there was a noticeable odor starting to develop underneath the canvas because of the heat. I told the attendants to burn the tent because the blood and dry skin would make it unusable. I went to the office and had Yvonne call Robert Lawson. She was able to get the call placed right away and Robert was on the phone.

"Hello David, did you find Chifungwe and get him put down?" he asked.

I quickly explained the events after he left and asked if he could fly to Fort Jameson tomorrow and bring the camera with him that I gave to the Game Guard observer.

"I can come tomorrow morning and will be there by eight A.M.," he said.

"Also, Robert, I need to fly along the escarpment to see if we can find Chifungwe again. While I had him down I painted a white patch on his back, so we should be able to see the spot from the air. Will we be able to do all this without refueling?" I asked

"No, I think it best to top off the tank when I land at Fort Jameson, then we will be okay to go into the Reserve and back to the airport, so I will see you in the morning."

With this information I said goodbye and hung up the telephone.

Chapter Fifteen

I went to Stan's office to discuss the events and how to proceed. We agreed that Yvonne would take me to the airport, and when Robert arrived I would unload the film and give it to her. She would bring the film back and give it to Stan. Stan would meet the regular airline flight at 10:30 A.M. and direct the flight attendant to carry the film to Lusaka. He would then radio CGO at the scheduled time and ask him to have a courier from the Game Department meet the Zambian Airways flight from Fort Jameson to retrieve the film box from the flight attendant. The courier would take the film to a photo shop that does contract work for the Game Department and wait for the slides to be developed. The courier would return the slides to CGO who would then view them on the screen to see if the license plate number was readable. The CGO would then let the Minister know of the incident and also call Commissioner Musonda to give him any results taken from the photographs.

We left the runway at approximately 8:30 A.M. and increased our altitude to 6,000 feet and flew toward Mpika. The flying time was less than one hour. We descended to 4,000 feet as we crossed the Munyamadzi River and then headed south along the Muchinga escarpment. We saw many family groups and lots of single elephants, but none had the white spot on its back. For the next hour we checked out many single elephants and did not have any luck.

The assumption was that Chifungwe would keep on the track that he was following yesterday and that was southwest from where he was immobilized. But what if he had done this only for a short period of time and then went in the opposite direction toward the area where we first caught him with the capture gun? Robert headed northeast, crossed the Munyamadzi Corridor, and was at the south edge of the North Luangwa Reserve when we saw a white spot at the edge of Pande Plain. Robert dropped in altitude and lowered his flaps to slow down as we flew over the elephant, and sure enough, it was Chifungwe. He seemed to be just fine and had been pulling branches off a mopane when he turned toward the noise and thrust his ears forward. The sun was at his back and just for a fleeting moment I thought I could even see the hole in his ear.

"Okay Robert, its time to go home," I said, and we headed for Fort Jameson.

When we arrived at the airport, Yvonne was there to meet us and to give me a message to call CGO the first thing in the morning. I thanked Robert and asked if I could rent his plane for a few days the next week.

"Of course you can rent my plane, but I would rather sell it to you," he said as he climbed into the cockpit, got seated, and shouted "Clear." The engine started and he was on his way to Mpika.

When we arrived back at the Game Department office I had Yvonne put a call in to Chilanga. My luck today seemed to be going well because the operator got through on the first try.

"Hello Owen, I hope you have good news," I said.

"I sure do. I have a color enlargement of the slide showing the license plate on the Land Rover. We can clearly see the number but none of the faces are visible—the passengers are too far inside the vehicle.

"I had the number checked through vehicle registration, and the Land Rover belongs to an employee of the Chinese Embassy in Lusaka," Owen said. "The Minister called the embassy, and they told him that the employee had gone on vacation with a friend from Tanzania. The vehicle was not registered with the Foreign Diplomatic Corp. It is the owner's personal vehicle and does not belong to the embassy.

"My guess is that the Tanzanian is also an embassy employee as they seem to be traveling together because of having connections with the railroad project. This whole issue has been given to a higher level by our director and will be handled through the Minister's Office because it involves two people with diplomatic status.

"Except for Joshua's involvement, we will not have any input to the investigation other than to provide what information we can to the Minister," Owen said.

Robert called the Game Department the next morning and left a message for me that he had to be in Fort Jameson on business all day Thursday and if I still wanted to use his Cessna I should meet him at 8:30 A.M. I went to the airport at the time he had suggested, and I arrived as he was walking through the gate to the terminal. He had come a little early to top off the tank, and the plane was ready to go.

"I will be here for about three hours, and you can use the Cessna during this period if it meets your needs," Robert said.

"I just want to make a short trip to the South Reserve for a look at the Valley from the air and maybe a last chance of seeing Chifungwe before he loses his white spot," I said. "Since I will be using your plane, you can use my Toyota and also you can charge the aircraft fuel to my account."

Robert got in the Toyota and drove off toward Fort Jameson, and I got in the Cessna and took off toward the South Reserve. It was a clear day with no wind and the ride was smooth. My course took me over Mfuwe, and I headed southwest toward the escarpment to an area where, several days ago, a Game Guard had reported that he had seen Spider. Today I did not forget my camera, and I had a Nikon with color slide film and our Bronica with black-and-white print film. I also had the aerial photograph that showed the secret spot that I was not supposed to know about. Out of curiosity it was my intention today to see this geologic formation from the air since it was along the route that I had to go to find Spider. The formation was easy to spot and I made a 360-degree slow turn to look at detail. Physical features on aerial photographs are somewhat exaggerated, and the actual geologic formation on the ground was not too interesting. My curiosity was satisfied, and after the turn I continued on the course.

The vegetation below was open mopane, and visibility was good. I saw many elephants but nothing that even came near having ivory that would be called a trophy or in the 100-pound class. After about thirty minutes of flying a grid pattern, I decided that today was not my day to see Spider, and I headed north toward the corridor. Water was still gushing out of the escarpment creating Mutinondo Falls, and this was an impressive sight. I took several slide shots with the idea that sometime I would enlarge the best one for a framed photograph. I turned to fly over the Chifungwe Plain where there were many herds and scattered single elephants. The number of elephants that I had seen from on the ground and in the air now exceeded thirty thousand. My thoughts took me back to the one elephant in the Columbus Zoo and how different it was seeing them in the wild, free to roam in a place of their own choosing either as singles or family groups. I spent another thirty minutes checking out single elephants for a white spot on its back, but it was nowhere to be found.

It was now time for me to start back to the airport, and I decided to follow the Munyamadza all the way to its confluence with the Luangwa. In flying this route I counted more than forty villages not far from the river and the number of huts and people was more than I had envisioned. I was again impressed by how important this area was for both wildlife and people. Somehow the government and particularly the Game Department had to resolve the conflicts of wildlife and humans that existed in the corridor and in a way that both could benefit, but this would be a major challenge. I reached the confluence without seeing an elephant with a white spot on its back and accepted the fact that I would not see Chifungwe again.

I crossed the Luangwa and headed for Fort Jameson and with just about enough time left not to keep Robert waiting. I was headed on the downwind leg to the runway when in front of me at my elevation was a vulture. In most cases in this situation the vulture will go down when you get near each other, but in this instance it did not and my tricycle landing gear hit the vulture. When I got to the airport I called the tower to take a look at my landing gear as I made a flyby. After two looks the tower operator said that everything appeared okay but that I should make a full flap landing at slow speed. I made a turn for the final approach and slowed down to just above stall speed. When my wheels hit the dirt and the plane slowed, the nose dropped and everything stayed in place. I taxied to the terminal, and Robert had just arrived. We both looked at the landing gear and nothing was damaged, but there was a dent in the wheel cover. I had the fuel truck fill the tanks and gave the key back to Robert and asked him to send me a bill for the flight time. He thanked me for the use of the Toyota and handed me the keys. I told him that I would keep him informed about the investigation on the attempt to poach Chifungwe. As he got into his Cessna and took off, I got into the Toyota and started for Fort Jameson. It was only a couple of minutes when I heard the plane over me. It wiggled its wings and then nosed upward, headed for Mpika. This was the last time that I saw Robert Lawson.

For several weeks Stan and Police Commissioner Musonda worked on getting information about Joshua Njovo. The local UNIP chairman told them that Joshua had been making occasional trips with his people to Mpika on the weekends. While there on party business, Joshua had met several of the railroad employees. When they found out that he worked with the Game Department, he became friends with a Chinaman and Tanzanian who were working on the railroad to Tanzania. The Chinaman paid Joshua to be an informer about the schedules of the anti-poaching unit in the Luangwa Valley and, in particular, information on the location of the elephant with the red ear. This accounted for the extra money that Joshua seemed to have from time to time that he could not have obtained from his current job with the Luangwa Survey. His involvement also explained why he had such an interest in seeing the map in my office that documented the movements of Chifungwe. The information about Joshua came from his close friends in UNIP and not from the Chinese Embassy.

Stan also found out that Joshua was providing information to Ian Finch, the hunting guide who disliked the cropping scheme in the South Reserve. On occasion Joshua would share with UNIP members money that he had been given by the Chinaman. This allowed him to brag about his "status" and was, of course, done as a bribe to keep them quiet about his activities in Mpika.

The Ministry for Parks and Tourism in Lusaka contacted the two embassies for information on the men in the Land Rover registered to the Chinaman. Both embassies said that their employees were on leave and had not returned to work. The Chinaman and Tanzanian were never seen again working on the railroad project, and the Land Rover was confiscated by the Game Department after it remained unused for several months while parked in Mpika.

Ian Finch lost his guide license because he was charged with obstructing Game Department employees in carrying out their official duties. As a result of losing his license, Ian left Zambia and started a hunting guide service in Tanzania.

Laston still lived in his village at Kazembe and never tired of telling people about his experience with the "gray ghost" with the red ear that glowed at night. The Game Department was not able to connect him with the Chinaman, Tanzanian, or Joshua because none of the local villagers or UNIP members were willing to provide the necessary information and he was not charged with poaching.

My assignment with FAO ended, and I returned to the United States to resume my position as a Wildlife Research Biologist for the U.S. Forest Service. The day I left Fort Jameson my two Game Guards, Sam Mlenga and James Ngulwe, came to my house to give me an elephant hair bracelet. They had cut the stiff hair from the tail of Chifungwe on the two occasions that we had him immobilized, but I was not aware that they had done this.

"This bracelet will bring you good health and happiness, and when you look at it you will remember James and me," Sam said.

"We will not forget you because no other person has ever treated us as equals like you have," James said.

I accepted the bracelet and told them that my experience with the two of them, along with other Africans in the Game Department, taught me many things about myself, but more importantly I learned that basically man and his desires are the same everywhere—only his environment and life circumstances are different. Having said that, I asked both of them to hold out their left wrist and I attached Timex watches that I had bought for them in Lusaka.

I left Africa knowing that our team had submitted a good report that documented the need for a UNDP project that would benefit the people of the Luangwa Valley and the Republic of Zambia. Several months later the project was fully funded and would last for five years.

When I boarded the same Dakota to leave Fort Jameson that brought my family and me from Lusaka to Fort Jameson, I stopped on the last step and turned to look back at the countryside. I thought to myself, *Someday I will return to Africa again on a different assignment—but that's another story.*

In the Munyamadzi Corridor near the Chifungwe Plain, if the light is right in the evening, you might see an elephant with a small hole in its left ear. Some Bisa people say that this elephant at one time had magical powers but the power was lost when a white man put him to sleep and took away his magic.